SUBURBS OF THE UNDERWORLD

AN ANTHOLOGY OF SHORT HORROR

Cyrus G. Oliver II

Bianfu Studios Press

Suburbs of the Underworld
Published by Bianfu Studios Press.
Copyright © 2017 Cyrus G. Oliver II
All rights reserved.
Cover art by Namira 'Rovateau' Salsabila with
background art by Deshen Adiguna.
First Edition, 2017
ISBN-10: 0-9984049-1-8
ISBN-13: 978-0-9984049-1-2

DEDICATION

This book is for anyone who has ever heard a bump in the night and lived to tell the tale.

CONTENTS

VISIT FROM A MONSTER

Noel Alistir was a dreamer. He had been from the time he was a child. Unlike his peers, though, he didn't dream of his future or of fame. Such things were out of his interest. He dreamed of something far more ingrained.

He dreamed of monsters. Often.

Not the usual types of monsters, either. Not shadowy men with red eyes. Not carnivorous leviathans, nor bloodthirsty apparitions. The monsters he dreamed of spoke clearly without speaking. These monsters did not hide in the dark. They had no claws, no contractible pathogens, no disembodied moans.

They had intentions.

Desires.

He tried to delineate the monsters from his mind, through both descriptions and illustrations, but his words and pictures were unintelligible to anyone except himself. After reliving the same dismissive dialogue with friends and family enough times, he dropped the subject entirely.

But the dreams intensified over time, until one fateful night when they finally stopped. Noel remembered it vividly. He was only seven years old at the time. It was shortly after his infant brother was born.

As Noel lay silently in bed, alone in his room, he heard what can only be described as the sound of a metronome — clicking slowly at first, then rapidly increasing in rhythm. He peered towards his bedroom door. The sound wasn't coming from inside his room, but from somewhere else, either the hallway or... the baby's room.

The clicking sound soon transformed into the beating of a drum accompanied by coordinated cracking of sticks and an occasional tinkling of wind chimes. Finally, the music (if you could call it that) was met with guttural chanting. Upon hearing it, a normal person would assume it was all the sounds of an ancient tribal ritual.

Then… the sound of a baby crying. It was Noel's brother. Instantly, the music stopped. The cries of his brother grew louder and louder. Noel climbed out of his bed and walked to his door. His brother was wailing and choking on his own screams at this point. Before Noel could open it, his door blew wide open. Startled, Noel jumped back. Almost back to his bed. Yet the only one at the doorway was his brother, lying on his back on the floor, still squirming and crying.

"Mom! Dad! Jacob's out of his crib!" Noel shouted. As usual, they didn't hear him. Suddenly Jacob went silent. The quietness felt eerie, it was less comforting than the crying. Noel looked at his baby brother's face. It looked as though he was in a trance. His eyes were entirely fixated on the stucco ceiling. Noel looked up, but he saw nothing out of the ordinary. He picked Jacob up and carried him back to the crib, lulling him back to sleep along the way.

After putting Jacob in the crib, Noel heard a noise coming from his bedroom. A knocking noise. He wanted to jump in the crib with Jacob, but a force was compelling him to investigate. He walked out into the hallway and peeked at his bed from a distance. It looked normal. Maybe the noise was just — wait. There was something on the bed. Something small and white.

It moved.

But just barely.

Noel stared, trying to make out what it was. It started to move again. It was some kind of animal, and it was struggling to breathe. Noel walked inside his room, his eyes glued to the creature on his bed. He lowered his body, sitting on his knees, to get a better view.

The creature… it was… a bird. And its wings were bleeding. Although its face lacked the same features of a human, the bird also appeared to be in a trance-like state. It writhed around on the bed for a few more moments, chirping quietly and incoherently, before puffing its entire body up, then slowly deflating and dying anticlimactically.

Noel stood up and gazed down at the corpse.

Then, he felt a presence. Something was at the doorway. It cast no shadow, but he knew it all the same. This was its grand entrance. The monster had arrived. Well, not arrived, it had been there all along. It had decided to show itself. Noel was nearly frozen in fear, his heart felt like it was about to burst from his chest, but just as he had felt drawn to enter his room before, so he felt drawn to turn around and face the monster.

Gradually, he turned his body sideways, then his head followed. And there it was. Waiting for him. Were those feet, or hooves? Was that an abdomen, or a thorax? Somehow it looked less real in reality than in his dreams.

His gaze worked all the way up the monster's hairless body. He didn't have enough time or focus to count all of its appendages and limbs. For all he knew it had eight fingers, but that wasn't what he wanted to see nor what it wanted him to see.

It wanted him to see its face.

At first, his arachnophobia convinced him it had the face of a spider — two protruding fangs and eight glistening, soulless eyes. But as his vision cleared, it looked more like the face of a crow. Or a mountain goat. Or a deformed old woman. Like a kaleidoscope, it seamlessly transitioned from one to the next. Maybe its face didn't matter after all. Maybe that was the point.

The monster pointed directly at Noel. Their destinies were intertwined. The dreams would finally be going away.

And they would be replaced by nightmares.

THE RED ENVELOPE

The bait was set. It had been for a long time. Unfortunately, living in the rural countryside of an already tiny region made the hunt even more difficult. For years, the elderly couple had sat it outside, just beside the dirt road leading out of the cemetery near their run-down house, hoping that someone would come.

Would take the bait.

Would take the... red envelope.

Cars passed by for years without stopping. Cyclists and even the occasional jogger carried on, passing the envelope without so much as a glance. Until finally a rainy day forced a driver to pull onto the shoulder of the road and wait out a storm.

The driver was Asa Peng, a freshman at university with a bright future ahead of him. He was a kind and trusting young man whose intelligence would surely take him far in life. And on that rainy day, Asa Peng spotted a bright red envelope lying in a wet ditch outside of his car.

After some hesitation, Asa decided to investigate. He retrieved the soggy envelope and took it back to his car. Despite its condition from being out in the elements of nature, it looked fancy. A gold-color stamp sealed its contents. Asa had no choice but to open it. Inside, he saw something that he would never forget.

Money. Lots of money. There had to have been at least $5,000 in cash inside. More than enough to pay off debts to his parents and then some.

This has to be a mistake, he thought. He figured

somebody must have accidentally dropped it, or the wind carried it there. Regardless, he knew he couldn't keep such a large amount of someone else's money.

When the rain let up, he drove further down the road, looking for a Lost & Found or anyone who might know who the envelope's owner was. There was only one house in the vicinity that looked occupied. He slowly drove up the weed-infested driveway, if you could even call it a driveway, and to the porch. An old couple sat outside. The woman was peeling skin off of strange-looking vegetables while the old man watched Asa intently.

Asa rolled his car window down.

"Excuse me, do either of you know anyone who this might belong to?" he queried as he raised the red envelope and pointed at it.

The old man's eyes beamed as his face produced a toothless smile.

"Yours! Yours!" he said gleefully.

"Mine? No, it's not mine. I just found it on the side of the road."

"Yours! Yours!" the old man exclaimed as he nudged his wife and motioned towards Asa. Upon seeing the envelope, she also lit up and began laughing before joining in her husband's chorus. "Yours! Yours! Yours!"

Asa was confused. Maybe they didn't understand. He took out some of the money to show them.

"It's not mine. It has money in it." he explained.

The old woman who had been sitting down was now by Asa's car window. She cupped his hand in her own, as he held the money, and folded it into a fistful of cash, patting it firmly.

"Yours." she said convincingly. The old man stood behind her, smiling and nodding.

"Oh. Okay. Thank you." Asa complied and tucked the red envelope into his coat pocket.

The old couple slowly backed away and went inside their house. Although they were out of sight, he still got the feeling they were watching him. Very confused and slightly unnerved, he pulled out of their driveway and continued home with the envelope and all of its contents, totally unaware of everything it contained.

As soon as he arrived back at his apartment, he took all the cash out of the envelope. His parents would surely be pleased to see him pay off his debts so soon. But something else came out with the cash. Something was tangled up and wrapped around it, something he hadn't noticed before.

It was hair.

Jet black hair.

And it looked unclean. Clumps of dirt held its roots together. Where had it come from? Asa had no idea. He untangled it from the money and discarded it into the kitchen waste bin. He had found the envelope outside, after all. There was no telling how long it had been out there and where the hair could have come from. Its presence wasn't given a second thought.

That night, as Asa lay in bed, he heard a noise. A scratching noise. It was coming from his bathroom door. It almost sounded like a dog was trapped inside, trying to claw its way out.

Nervously, he opened the door.

He peeked his head inside.

He saw… nothing. Other than the toilet, mirror, sink, and tub, the bathroom was empty.

Returning to his bed, Asa lay down once more. Before long, the noise started again and continued throughout the rest of the night.

It must be the wind, Asa thought to himself.

In the morning, Asa had to pee. It had been a long night. Sitting on the toilet, he looked at the door. Deep cuts and scratch-marks ran down its wooden surface. From top to bottom, it appeared as though something had been clawing at the door with sharpened claws for hours.

Shocked, he quickly emptied his bladder and zipped up his pants. Before leaving, he looked down at the waste bin. Something familiar was inside.

The dirt-covered hair from the day before.

He was sure he had thrown it away in the kitchen. Yet there it was in the bathroom trash. Something sinister had transpired, but Asa didn't know what.

He could feel somebody or something watching him. It was the same feeling he felt outside of the old couple's home. A lot of unsettling things were happening and it was just the beginning of the day. Asa dare not wait for any more surprises. Without hesitation, he left for class. He left so quickly that he forgot his backpack – textbooks and all.

None of that mattered though.

He just wanted to get away.

In class, he couldn't focus at all. All he could think about was that scratching sound from the night before.

Crrr…

Crrr…

Crrrrrrr…

And that hair.

That dark black hair.

Who did it belong to? Why was it in the envelope? And most importantly to Asa, what would happen to him if he returned to his apartment for another night? As he walked to yet another class, he pondered these questions. In the next classroom, he saw something that stopped him dead in his tracks. Something sitting on his usual chair.

It was his backpack. The one he had forgotten to bring. He stared at it for a few moments that felt more like a few hours before opening it up. Sure enough, it was indeed his. His textbooks. His notes. His handwriting.

But how? He didn't have any roommates. There was no one who could have possibly brought it to campus for him.

No one except… that thing. That thing from the bathroom. That thing that had spent all of the previous night defacing the door, trying to scratch its way out.

Now it *was* out. Clearly. And following him.

Asa decided not to go back to his apartment; instead, he would spend the night at his parent's house. It wouldn't take much explaining. His mother would just be glad to have him visit, even if just for a night.

Maybe he could call a monk or an exorcist to rid his home of... whatever *it* was. Until then, he didn't feel comfortable stepping foot back in that apartment, let alone the building itself.

Just as he expected, it didn't take any convincing for his parents to welcome him into their home. They gave him the traditional hugs and support as they always did. The same support that had given him the motivation to succeed as much as he had. To get accepted into the top university in the country.

Unfortunately, that motivation and support did nothing for him now. Behind his forced smile was a very scared young man. The worst part was that he didn't even know what he was scared of. He just knew that he wanted a good night's sleep.

As darkness signaled the beginning of a new night, Asa went to his old bedroom while his parents went to theirs. Once again, he stiffly lay down in his bed and closed his eyes.

Once again, he heard a sound. This time it wasn't the sound of scratching.

It was the sound of something else entirely.

Something far more disconcerting.

He heard the disembodied sound of crying. A woman crying, specifically. It started off low, but gradually increased in volume. There was no doubt that this sound was real. And that it was coming from a vent in his room.

"Mom, is that you?" he questioned out loud. But there was no response. The sound of weeping just continued without pause.

Then, an even worse sound was heard. The sound of the vent opening.

CLANG!

Asa shot upright. He looked directly at the vent. Its cover had fallen to the floor, leaving the rectangular aperture completely open.

Now he could hear the crying even more profoundly. It echoed throughout his entire room. He put his hands over his ears to shield them from the piercing wail.

Finally, the crying stopped.

He slowly lowered his guard, hands to his side.

He stared at the open vent.

Something caught his eye.

It was faint, but noticeable. Two white orbs glowing in the darkness of the vent. If he didn't know better, Asa would assume the two circles made out the shape of two eyes staring back at him.

He could hear heavy breathing coming from the vent now. It almost sounded like a disturbed cat growling deeply. After an intense stare-down between Asa and the orbs, the vent cover seemingly lifted itself up, hovered above the floor, and screwed itself back over the opening in the wall.

It goes without saying, but Asa didn't sleep at all that night. The following morning, over breakfast, he told his parents something had happened to the vent in his bedroom.

Curious, his father went to inspect it. After a few minutes, his father returned to the table.

"The vent seems fine," he said. "But it's a bit dirty. That sometimes causes strange sounds. You know, as the house settles."

"How dirty was it?" Asa queried.

"Not much. Just had some hair inside."

"Hair? How would hair get in the vent?" Asa could feel sweat begin to slide down his forehead.

"I don't know," his father responded with a grin as he lifted up a handful of long black hair covered in mud. "Maybe it's yours! Yours! Yours! Yours!"

Asa's mother laughed.

"Yours! Yours! Yours!" she chimed.

Asa looked at his parents' distorted faces. They almost resembled the old couple he had seen on that rainy day when he found the red envelope. They slowly ambled towards him with devilish grins on their faces as they repeated "yours, yours, yours" over and over again.

He walked backwards and bumped into the kitchen counter, knocking over cereal boxes and medicine bottles, before falling to the floor.

His father threw a big wad of the hair on him. He could feel strands of it wrapping around his throat.

Ripping the tentacles of hair-locks off his neck, Asa threw it back onto the floor and scurried out of the kitchen. He ran for the front door, nearly tripping over his own feet and furniture along the way.

He slammed into the door, before flinging it open and running outside to his car. As he started the ignition, he could see his parents looking out the window at him. But he knew they were only his parents in appearance.

Mere shells of their former selves. Whatever was inside them now was not the mother and father he knew and loved.

With the turn of a key and the slam of a pedal, Asa quickly sped out of the driveway and down the street as far away from his own family as possible. He dared not look in the rear-view mirror. Instead, he opened the glove compartment and shuffled through its contents. Old bills and magazines spilled onto the floor. Then he finally felt what he was searching for.

An envelope. The red envelope. Seemingly, it was the cause of all these events.

He had to go back to the countryside. Back to that dirt road where he found the envelope. Maybe, he thought, if he returned the envelope to that place, everything would be normal again.

For hours, Asa drove. He drove until the sun set and the sky went pitch dark. Although the rural road wasn't far from the city and he had driven down it many times before, for some reason he had difficulty finding it. It was as if something was taunting him, forcing him to drive in circles.

Finally, his car headlights revealed a familiar sight: a cemetery next to an old house. This was the house where he met the old couple a few days prior. It had always looked shabby, but now it was fully dilapidated. There was no way anyone occupied it. It looked like it had been abandoned for years if not decades.

Where should he put the envelope? Back in the ditch beside the road? In the weed-infested driveway of the old house?

While agonizing over what to do next, two orbs lit up in the cemetery. Despite being faint, their glow was in direct contrast to the darkness of the night, making them stand out noticeably. Asa locked his doors and watched. He recognized the orbs. Or rather, eyes. The same eyes from the vent.

The eyes floated past gravestones and towards his car. As they got closer, a shape began to form around them.

It was the shape of a ghostly apparition.

A woman.

She was wearing a wedding dress. Her eyes, glowing ever brighter. Her skin, a translucent white that matched her dress.

She walked slowly, but with an otherworldly confidence. She was coming for Asa.

Asa quickly rolled down his window and hurled the red envelope into the tall grass; then, he put his car into reverse. But the car stalled.

His headlights started to flicker and his car radio began playing a terrifying melody of white noise.

The woman was only a few feet away from his car now.

"Please! You have your money! I'm sorry! Whatever I did, I'm sorry! Just leave me alone, I beg you!" Asa pleaded manically, tears running down his face and spittle projecting from his panicked mouth.

Suddenly, the woman disappeared.

The headlights were restored to their normal state.

The radio played a soft pop song.

Asa could feel his heart beating fast. It felt like it was about to burst from his chest. His body was stiff with fear. It took him a few moments to compose himself and gather the courage to look around. When he did, the ghost was nowhere to be seen.

Gradually, his heart rate slowed down to its regular pace. He breathed a sigh of relief. Apparently, all he had to do was simply return the envelope. His plan had worked.

His horrible ordeal was finally over. He could go back to being a model student. He could go back to the old life he knew so well not even a week ago.

Life was good.

He closed his eyes and reclined in his seat to unwind.

Then, he felt a gentle breeze caress his face. *The wind sure is cool tonight,* he thought.

It wasn't the wind though. When he opened his eyes, Asa saw a woman looking back at him. She was standing outside his window. Hunched over, she was the one caressing his face.

Before he could react, the woman leaned in for a kiss at lightning speed. With each painful tightening of her lips, she sucked the life out of him until only dust remained.

Standing beside two gravestones off in the distance, an old couple watched with satisfaction.

"The dowry was a bit much. Was he really worth $5,000?" the old woman said to her husband.

"It's fine. The important thing is our little girl finally

found a suitable groom." the old man responded gruffly. With that, they both faded into the night.

KASA-OBAKE

The pitter-patter of rain sounded off the top of an open umbrella. Tracing down the umbrella's handle were the soft hands of Azami Takahashi. She was walking to the house of her secret lover, Kazuo. Actually, it was Kazuo's parent's house, but they were out of town tonight, as they so often were. Although Azami had only been dating Kazuo for a few weeks, she was deeply in love with him. As high school students, he had convinced her to keep their love strictly confidential. It was his one condition: their relationship could not be made public. It would cause too much drama, he told her, both in their private and academic lives among family, friends, and peers.

His logic was sound enough. Not that it needed to be logical, she would have agreed to any condition he set, no matter how extreme. The fact that it was such a simple request made it even more agreeable.

She had offered to bring him a freshly cooked dinner this night, but he ordered she only bring one thing.

Herself.

Just the way he had commanded her, so smooth and confident, made her heart race with excitement. She didn't know much, but she knew she loved Kazuo and she hoped he loved her too. She thought he did, anyway.

Upon her arrival at his house, he greeted her. Not with a hug or peck on the cheek, but with a wave for her to hurry inside. His apathy would have concerned her if she didn't trust him so much. *Whatever his reason for being slightly indifferent towards my presence must be a good one,* she thought. He probably just wanted her to get out of the rain quickly. He was so thoughtful and considerate.

Once inside Kazuo's house, Azami folded her umbrella.

"Put it over there." Kazuo instructed, pointing at an umbrella stand by the door.

Azami complied without a second thought. She didn't even bother putting it in with the handle sticking out, but instead placed it inside the stand handle first, with its top protruding out in an unsightly manner.

Kazuo didn't seem to notice.

"On your knees." he said, as he pulled out his smartphone with the camera pointed directly at her.

Azami had always known Kazuo to be an assertive young man, it was partly why she liked him so much, but she hadn't expected this. He had never been so bullish before. Nonetheless, she didn't want to disappoint him. She submitted to his demand without resistance. And that was just the first demand of many that would follow that night.

After an hour into their time together, Kazuo finally stopped recording with his phone.

"I can't record any more. The memory is full." he sighed as he stretched his naked body. By now, both he and Azami were nude.

"I'm sorry. Are you happy?" Azami asked with genuine concern.

Before Kazuo could respond, three knocks were heard at the door.

"God, is that your parents?" Azami whispered fearfully.

"No. No. Shut up. Shhhhh!" Kazuo snapped at Azami, placing a single finger over her lips to signal her to be quiet. "I need you to go out the fire escape."

"Go out? But why? It's raining. And you said that's not your parents." It was the first time Azami had questioned him.

"Just… listen to me, all right? You can't be here right now, it's —"

"Kazuo? Are you home?" a timid voice asked from outside the door. It was the voice of a teenage girl. The doorknob frantically jiggled up and down and side to side.

"Who is she?" Azami questioned further, this time with more intensity.

Suddenly, the door opened and a girl wearing the same high school uniform as Azami entered the room. She was also wearing a scarf and striped leggings.

It was Azami's classmate, Miyuki.

She was looking downward while shaking the rain off her hands.

"I just remembered, you gave me a —" Miyuki looked up and saw Kazuo and Azami naked together on the couch. "—key."

"Miyuki?"

"Azami?"

Both girls stared at each other for a moment, then looked at Kazuo.

"Kazuo, what is she doing here?" they both asked in

unison.

"Miyuki… I'm so sorry." he said, choking back tears. "This girl, Azami, look, she's nothing."

First, Azami couldn't believe what she saw, another girl – her own classmate no less – walking in on her during a private moment with the boy she loved; now, she couldn't believe what she heard, the boy she loved telling said girl that she – Azami – was nothing.

Kazuo stood up, wrapped a blanket around his waist, and walked towards Miyuki with open arms, abandoning poor Azami on the couch. Miyuki embraced him with tears in her eyes.

"How could you, Kazuo?!" she cried, "You dummy!"

"I'm sorry, baby. Please forgive me. I'll do anything you want, anything at all."

Azami watched as the boy she loved hugged another girl and not only comforted her, but now promised to do anything for her. That was the promise she had been expecting for herself. Instead, now she was left alone with nobody to console her. The only consolation she had was to currently be subjected to the humiliation of being rejected and having a front-row seat to watch the aftermath.

She stood up from the couch and gathered her clothes. She, too, had worn her school uniform. Slowly, she put it back on.

Miyuki and Kazuo were still deep in conversation as he tried to explain himself. It looked as though Miyuki was buying it. Certainly, if this was a competition, she was the clear winner. Not only did she have a key to

Kazuo's parent's house, but now she had his full attention.

Azami cleared her throat.

"Kazuo." she said in such a plain matter that it cut through all other noises and distractions.

He and Miyuki simultaneously paused and looked at Azami. She stammered to the reunited couple with her head down in an effort to hide the mix of emotions her face was processing.

"Kazuo… I…" Azami stretched out her right arm. "I hate you!"

Her arm swung fiercely as her hand slapped Kazuo's smug face. Immediately, Miyuki jumped into action. Kazuo may have been a lecherous cheater, but he was her lecherous cheater and she wouldn't allow anyone other than herself to dole out retribution against him for his crimes. Least of all, someone she saw as less than nothing, someone like Azami.

"How dare you touch my future husband!" she screamed, shoving Azami. The shove was forceful enough to knock Azami off her balance and send her free-falling towards the umbrella stand where her umbrella – top up – was sitting.

She fell with her body's full weight accelerating her collapse towards the outwardly positioned umbrella top.

Slurck!

The umbrella had fully penetrated through her back and pierced through her chest on the other side. Impaled, she looked down and saw a patch of blood begin to pool around the wound. The pool turned into an ocean as the blood hemorrhaged at an incredible speed, drenching her uniform in red and soon covering most of the entrance's tiled floor within range of her dying body.

"Azami!" Kazuo shouted helplessly.

Miyuki just watched in disbelief.

"Azami!"

Azami looked up at Kazuo with eyes that were soon to be dead. The life was visibly draining from them each passing second.

"Kazuo." she managed to gasp, with blood running down the sides of her mouth. "I hate you."

With those final words, Azami vomited projectile blood.

Blurrrrrgth!

She then slumped over.

Miyuki and Kazuo gazed at Azami's fresh corpse for what felt like an eternity. Was this the same warm body that had been pressed against Kazuo on the couch not too long ago? Was this the same girl who had been so happy to come inside from the rain earlier tonight? Reality began to sink in as they both absorbed what had just transpired. Miyuki had murdered Azami. It was she who pushed her to her demise. And Kazuo. He had watched, nay, facilitated this event through his own insensitive actions. Insensitive was an understatement. And now. Now Azami was dead. No doctor could save her now.

Finally, Kazuo spoke, breaking the silence.

"Go to the bathroom. There's bleach in the cabinet under the sink."

"But–"

"Go!"

Miyuki scampered to the bathroom and began shifting through the lower cabinet just as Kazuo had directed.

"Bring back some towels, too! We need to clean this... mess."

He knelt down on the floor, not to dissimilar from the way Azami had knelt down before him earlier, and he peered into her lifeless eyes. Somehow they seemed to be peering back at him. With intent. An angry intent. He couldn't bear her gaze, so he attempted to close her eyelids, but they slowly slid back open and stared deep into his soul.

Kazuo couldn't stand for it any longer. While waiting for cleaning supplies, he pressed his thumbs deep under each of Azami's dead eyes and shoveled them out one after the other. He threw them both in his dog's food bowl.

"Momo!" he called. "Momo! Dinner time!"

A Jack Russell Terrier bound into the room and licked up each eyeball. It took him a while to chew threw their rubbery texture, but they must have been delicious because he finished them off in no time and looked at Kazuo with expectant eyes as if he wanted more.

But Kazuo couldn't provide any more even if he had them, for now he had a body to dispose of. Miyuki entered the room with bleach and towels.

"What happened to her eyes?"

"Never mind that. Toss me a towel."

The two of them spent the rest of the night mopping up blood with fresh towels and scrubbing red off the tiled floor. Luckily for them, none of it touched the carpet.

By the time it was morning, all they had left to do was hide the body. Unable to carry it out in broad daylight, they decided to buy themselves some time and swaddled it up with plastic wrap before placing it in the deep freezer in his parent's basement. His parents wouldn't be home for at least a few more days, and nobody else knew about his relationship with Azami. If he and Miyuki went to class, nobody would suspect either of them of her disappearance. They could decide where to toss her body later.

After they left for school, they completely forgot to throw away one more piece of evidence.

The umbrella.

When they had removed it from Azami's corpse to wrap her up in plastic, they simply discarded it in the sink, planning to rinse it off and throw it away later. As they walked to the subway to go to school, it still sat in the sink, dripping with blood.

Momo the dog jumped onto the kitchen counter and walked to the sink. First, he sniffed the umbrella. Then, he began licking it, slurping up as much of the blood until it stained his doggy mouth. Suddenly, Momo felt a sharp pain in his snout. He had been bitten! And slowly but surely, his nose was being chewed down to a pulp.

It was the umbrella! A mouth full of razor-sharp teeth had materialized on the surface of its flaps, which was currently devouring Momo's face.

The little dog cried under muffled whines until his entire head was crushed and the base of his skull was totally severed from his spinal cord. Rising from the sink, the umbrella materialized yet another body part. A single snake-like eye centered above its newborn mouth. The umbrella swiftly opened itself, splattering both Momo and Azami's blood all over the kitchen walls. Then, by floating through a self-produced, invisible current of air, it began to glide through the house. Its destination: the basement.

The umbrella floated downstairs to the basement and landed standing upright. It looked at the deep freezer with its lone eye. A long tongue twisted out of its mouth and wrapped around the freezer handle. With a flick of its tongue it opened the freezer door and jumped onto the freezer's edge looking down at Azami's corpse.

The umbrella spoke with a deep, booming voice that reverberated throughout the room.

"Azami Takahashi. Dost thou wish to awaken?"

Azami's body was unresponsive. Frost had already started to form on the plastic wrapped around her.

"Azami Takahasi. Permit I to help thee and thou may avenge thineself most righteously."

Instantly, one of her arms twitched. Within a few seconds, her whole body was writhing in the plastic. One of her fingernails cut through the plastic and was able to create an opening that she tore through to escape. Soon, she was sitting up, feeling around her surroundings.

"My eyes... Kazuo took my eyes."

"Aye. His hound hath already supped on them. Worry not, for the hound is no longer. I vanquished it. And I will be thine eye from now on, if thou will have me."

"Who are you?"

"Ye can call me by mine given name. Kase-obake. I art the rainshade that pierced through thine body."

"Rainshade?"

"My apologies. These days ye might refer to my status as an umbrella."

"Wait. You're an umbrella? My umbrella? The one that impaled me?"

"'Tis so. The very same. But mine spirit dwells in all inanimate umbrellas, waiting to be called upon by those who seek vengeance. A vengeance many discarded umbrellas have felt for ages. The vengeance of the lost and forgotten. Vengeance that fuels a deep-seated hatred that pulsates through the living and non-living world. This same hatred coursed through thine blood yesternight, soaking deep into mine very fabric and calling me here."

"I still feel it. The hatred. Hatred for Kazuo. It's stronger now than any love I might have ever felt for him. He's a monster. Worse than a monster!"

"Aye. So what do ye say? Shall we torment him until his final moments in this life and thereafter?"

Azami didn't hesitate. "Yes," she nodded as brain matter could be seen through her empty eye sockets. "We shall."

"Excellent choice, Azami Takahashi. Hold still."

Kasa-obake unrolled more of his massive tongue from his mouth and wrapped it around Azami's body. She looked like a mummy covered with layers of tongue instead of linen cloth. After his saliva had saturated every inch of her, he unwrapped his tongue, rolling it back into his mouth.

"What did you just do?"

"I hath given thee new powers. Powers from the underworld. Ye may pass through both floors and walls, make thineself invisible to mortal eyes, and possess the bodies of thine enemies. Just to name a few."

Azami's skin glowed with a blue hue now. She looked like a proper ghost, but this was her body – except now it was in both a physical and non-physical state. Now she could cross between two planes of existence. Between the realm of the living and the realm of the dead. But something was still missing.

"I... I still can't see."

"Hold mine staff and see through mine eye."

Azami reached up and felt around. She grabbed hold of Kasa-obake's handle. His energy jolted through her. Immediately, her sense of sight was restored; not through her own eyes, though, but through his single eye. His eye was large enough to compensate for the fact he only had one. Actually, his one eye was far superior to the previous two eyes she used to own. His acted as a sort of wide lens, capable of scoping out an entire room at a single glance with perfect clarity.

"As long as ye hold mine staff, ye shall be granted with mine eyesight. Now, let us test thine powers."

Azami nodded then tightened her grip on Kasa-obake. She floated up and passed through the ceiling into the first floor of the house. Her murder scene.

"Thine phasing powers art impeccable." Kasa-obake said with pride, as though it was his own doing. To be fair, in some ways it was.

The sound of thunder cracked as lightning flashed outside, like a sign of Azami's rebirth. Dark clouds gathered over the neighborhood. Tonight would be another rainy night. And soon, Miyuki and Kazuo would arrive at home. Presumably, they'd be keen to finish what they started. To finish hiding a body that was no longer where they left it.

A resurrected body that was now capable of pushing back.

Of revenge.

Walking down the alley outside, Miyuki and Kazuo were trying to keep calm.

"Do you think anybody knows she's dead? Some people were asking where she was today." Miyuki worried out loud.

"Keep your voice down." Kazuo scolded. "Nobody will suspect a thing if we don't raise any red flags, like talking about it in public."

Kazuo shuffled his hands through his pockets, searching for his key to the house. He produced the key and walked towards the entrance. With a twist of the lock, both he and Miyuki were back home. As far as they knew, everything was as they left it.

"What are we gonna do with the body now?" Miyuki

cried.

"I'll handle it. But first. Get on your knees." Kazuo barked.

"But–"

"On your knees!"

Miyuki sobbed as she knelt down. Kazuo pulled out his camera.

"Now, you're going to do exactly as I say, or I'm going to tell everyone you murdered Azami."

Just as he was about to give his next order, Kazuo glanced over at the kitchen. He had to do a double take.

"Where did all that blood come from?" he muttered in stupefied awe.

"Ah! It's all over the walls!" Miyuki screamed.

Kazuo motioned for her to be silent. He walked to the kitchen and investigated. His eyes followed trails of blood leading back to the kitchen sink. On the counter was the rotting corpse of a decapitated dog.

"Momo!" he shouted. "What happened?!"

He dashed over to the counter.

"Who did this to you, Momo? Momo?!"

Then. Three knocks at the door.

Kazuo and Miyuki looked at each other with true fear in their eyes.

Three more knocks at the door.

"Should I go see who it is?" Miyuki whispered.

"Wait." Kazuo grabbed a baseball bat and walked over to the door. He looked out the peephole, but saw nobody outside. With the bat held behind his back, he opened the door. Again, no one was there. He closed the door.

"Weird." he said to himself.

Suddenly, Miyuki screamed. With a flash of lightning, a high school girl with blue skin and dark, empty eyes had appeared behind Kazuo holding an umbrella. As the flash from the lightning disappeared, so did the girl.

"What?! What happened?!"

Miyuki pointed with a shaking finger. Kazuo looked behind himself but nothing was there.

"I saw a girl!" Miyuki shrieked. "She was standing right behind you! Holding an umbrella! She was wearing a school uniform!"

Kazuo went pale.

"Come on. Let's get rid of that body. Now!"

He grabbed Miyuki's left arm and barreled down the stairs to the basement, dragging her along. As soon as his foot touched the basement floor, he froze. The deep freezer was open, as you already know.

Kazuo let go of Miyuki's arms, but she didn't move. They both gawked at the freezer. After swallowing a lump in his throat, Kazuo approached it. He slowly leaned over to look inside.

"H-how does she look? How's th-th-the body?" Miyuki stuttered.

Kazuo looked back at her.

"It's… gone."

Miyuki fell to the floor. Crying and shaking, as she was wont to do. Her knees bent together. Tear drops falling onto the concrete floor.

"Get up!" Kazuo shouted. "Get up, dammit!"

Lightning flashed again, and the high school girl with blue skin and dark, empty holes for eyes appeared once more. And once again, she was holding an umbrella. But this time she didn't disappear with the lightning. It was Azami. She stood firm, her eyes locked onto Kazuo and his, likewise, locked onto hers.

Miyuki trembled. She could only see Kazuo's face, but it was obvious he was staring death in the eyes. She slowly turned her neck to look behind. Standing behind her was the ghost of Azami Takahashi, who lowered her umbrella. An umbrella with a giant eye staring directly at Miyuki's face. Kasa-obake. His mouth grinned with rows of triangular shark teeth.

"Miss Takahashi, may I sup on this one?"

Azami nodded. "You may."

Just as Miyuki was about to scream, Kasa-obake's tongue lunged down her pretty little throat and ripped out her vocal cords.

"Mmm… quite an appetizer!" he chortled. "Now for the main course!"

Azami swung Kasa-obake at Miyuki's head like a golf club with a mouth. He devoured her head whole. A fountain of blood sprayed out her neck and onto Kazuo's face. Her headless body collapsed onto the floor.

"Sorry, let me get that for ye."

Kasa-obake stretched out his slithery tongue and used it to wipe the blood off of Kazuo's face, leaving behind a slimy residue.

"Azami…" Kazuo said, his voice shaking. "I'm sorry, baby. I tried to stop Miyuki, but she was too crazy. She meant nothing to me. You were the only girl for me, you always have been. That's why, last night, I invited you here instead of her."

He gave Azami a big hug.

"You were much better at taking orders. I wish she had been the one to die last night, instead of you."

If she could have, Azami would have cried. Her lack of tear ducts prevented her from doing so.

"You don't cry like she did either. She was so annoying." he added.

"Shall we finish this, Miss Takahashi?" Kasa-obake interrupted.

Azami stood motionless. Kazuo may have killed her. He may have destroyed her eyes. He may have led her on and cheated.

But there is only a thin line separating hate from love. And deep down, Azami loved Kazuo. He hadn't destroyed her heart.

Using one arm, she returned his hug,f while her other arm held on to her faithful umbrella. She kissed Kazuo on the lips, and he kissed her. He looked into her vacant eye sockets. Although just the sight of them made his stomach churn, he smiled.

"I love you, Azami." he said with all the sincerity he could muster.

Azami smiled back, then looked down at Miyuki's corpse.

"I win." she taunted.

HYBRID

Late one night, Antonio Diaz tended to his crops. A farmer by trade, he knew the importance of a hard day's work. His livelihood depended on it. But he also knew the sun was far too hot on a summer day in Brazil to accomplish much without inducing a heat stroke. So, he waited until night to plough the fields with his tractor as he had done many nights in the past.

But this night was different. A strange mood was in the air. He couldn't put his finger on it, but Antonio knew tonight was going to be special. He had no idea just how special it would be, but he started to get some idea when a bright star lit up the sky above him. To him, it looked like the star grew bigger and bigger, enveloping the darkness all around. He soon realized it wasn't growing, but was in fact approaching him.

It was no ordinary star. Its light nearly blinded him with its intensity as it hovered overhead. Now he saw it clearly. It was egg-shaped and increasing velocity. A red laser-light beamed from the craft and seemingly targeted him.

Antonio attempted to speed away on his tractor as the unidentified flying object drew nearer. If you've ever driven a tractor before, let alone ridden one, you'd know what an exercise in futility this would be. The tractor was no match for the craft in terms of speed or anything else.

Soon, the aerial craft landed in his field and was mere meters away from him.

As the UFO's light cast shadows from the stalks of

wheat, Antonio's tractor broke down. He then attempted to flee on foot, but was tackled by a humanoid being. It must've been only five feet tall and wore a gray uniform and helmet. Its bright blue eyes were the only things glistening from inside the helmet.

"■■■■■■■■■■■■■■■■■■■■■■■■■■■■■■■■■■■ ■■■■■■■■■■■!" it said in a language Antonio could not understand that resembled the sound of a dog barking. The creature held Antonio's arm behind his back as his face was shoved into the dirt. He felt like he was under arrest for a crime he didn't commit.

He struggled to look up, but when he did he saw three more beings join the first one. They each grabbed one of his limbs and dragged him on board their craft, barking to each other along the way.

Once inside, they shut the door behind them and led Antonio to a circular room with metal walls. Handling him like a chef might handle fresh meat that was to be thrown on a grill, they stripped Antonio of all his clothes and meticulously lathered every inch of his body with an unearthly gel.

After that, they shuffled him into yet another room. Fully naked, he confusedly looked on, watching as the beings closed the door in front of themselves, and simultaneously deserted him in the room with no one else.

Small nozzles poked out from the wall and began spraying a heavy odorless fog into the room's atmosphere. Antonio tried his best not to inhale it, but it was no use. He started to feel dizzy and lightheaded before vomiting all over the floor. Everything was hazy after that. The only clear memory he could recall later was that an unclothed woman entered the room after the fog subsided.

She was the epitome of beauty. Imagine a beautiful woman. Now multiply that image by a thousand, and you might be close to describing what this woman looked like. Her hair was a magnificent red. Her eyes were almost cat-like.

Antonio tried to make conversation with her, but she remained silent. She never responded. However, she did guide his hand and initiate what seemed like a mating ritual. That final initiation was the last thing he could remember.

Beyond that, Antonio's recollection was waking up in the field where he had been riding his tractor. When he woke up he was fully clothed again, but he had trouble standing. After a few attempts, he crawled back to his house on all fours where he proceeded to vomit some more.

The following day, police officers knocked on his door. They were responding to some reports from neighbors. Reports of witnessing strange goings-on in Antonio's field from the night before. Reports of bright lights, UFOs, and other commotion.

Antonio was apprehensive at first, but eventually relayed everything he had experienced to the officers. He spared no details, describing his abduction and time aboard the UFO. They transported him to the nearest hospital for both a physical and mental evaluation.

The doctors there could not verify everything he said was accurate, but they did notice his body had been exposed to high levels of radiation and many of his physical complaints were consistent with radiation sickness. Moreover, his psychological evaluation came back normal. He seemed to exhibit no signs of mental illness.

On his property, police found some evidence of foul play. There were impressions made in the soil of his field that suggested something had indeed landed there. There were also footprints leading away from and back to the impressions. Samples of the dirt in his field also revealed high levels of radiation.

Still, nothing could be done. Whatever had landed there was long gone, and with nothing stolen and no suspects to arrest, the case was largely filed away and considered unsolved after the media frenzy surrounding it subsided.

Antonio returned to his normal life and began to wonder how much of what he experienced was real, and how much of it, if any, was imaginary.

Being part of the blue-collar agricultural scene, it didn't take long for him to get back into the swing of things. He tried his best to move on, and mostly succeeded.

Other than recurring nightmares of being abducted by aliens, he suffered few setbacks or negative side effects.

That is, until a few years later when he heard a knock on his door early in the morning. Several police officers were waiting for him outside. When he opened the door, they explained that they might have a breakthrough in his case. They asked him to accompany them to the police station for questioning.

At the station, they brought him into a sealed room to meet a young girl. She looked to be about eight years old or so. Her eyes were large, almost like that of doll's. Her hair was blonde, yet thinning. She was wearing an over-sized white shirt that covered her entire body. For some reason, Antonio instantly felt a connection with her.

"Do you know this girl?" one of the officers asked.

[Tell them I'm your daughter.] a child's voice sounded off in Antonio's inner mind.

He looked directly at the girl and she looked back at him.

[Tell them.]

It was as though she was talking to him telepathically. Memories of the night when he was on board that strange craft flashed through his mind's eye.

"I know her. She's my daughter."

An officer leaned back against the wall and crossed his arms. "Really? Interesting to hear you say that. Farmers found her in a field last night. She doesn't have any identification on her and hasn't spoken to anyone since she's been found. Care to explain where she came from? Any birth certificate or other proof of relation?"

"You must have assumed we're related when you brought me here. I should be asking how you know, not the other way around."

"Just a hunch, Mr. Diaz. The last time we responded to a mysterious case about someone in a field, it was on your property and the someone was you. And we just got back test results showing this young lady's body holds similar levels of radiation to the levels measured in yours that night you claimed to have been abducted."

Antonio bit his lower lip and looked down to the floor. He could feel his heart pounding through his chest. This was a big deal. Something significant was happening, although he didn't know what.

The officer leaned down to Antonio's eye level, staring at him from across a wooden table.

"Mind if we take some blood samples from the girl?" he asked bluntly. "You know, to confirm you two are related?"

[You can't let him do that.] a voice inside Antonio's head said. He looked up at his 'daughter'. She offered him an intense stare. *[Don't let the man take my blood, Papa.]*

Antonio sat up and took a deep breath. "I'm sorry, officer. I can't allow that."

"Is that so?"

The officer nodded his head to signal he understood as he rested both hands on his hips and looked at the ceiling. Also taking a deep breath.

Suddenly, in a rage, he flipped over the table that Antonio had been sitting in front of, flinging it into the wall and breaking it into pieces. A tomato red color washed over his face as he pressed it against Antonio's and snarled. "I'm afraid I can't accept your answer, Mr. Diaz! Let me be frank with you! This girl – this thing –

your daughter – killed three of the finest officers on staff here! I don't know why, I don't know how, but she did. Their bodies are virtually unrecognizable. Spontaneously combusted into piles of gooey flesh!"

The officer wiped sweat from his brow. "Now. Forgive me for losing my cool. But some cooperation on your part would be greatly appreciated."

He slammed his hands down on each arm of Antonio's chair. "So… where did she come from?"

"I… I…"

Suddenly, the officer levitated in the air and slammed into the wall like the table he had just thrown. Two other guards in the room pulled out their guns, one pointing at Antonio and the other at the girl. Both weapons fired. But the bullets stopped in mid-air before shooting back at the center of both guards' heads. They collapsed in unison.

Antonio was visibly shaken. He looked at the girl in shock.

"Wh-what happened? Did you do that?"

The girl stood up and grabbed Antonio's right hand.

[Follow me.]

Her eyes glowed a bright white light that blinded Antonio when he looked into them. His entire surroundings became white as he was apparently being metaphysically transmitted to another location.

As his vision restored, he found himself in a heavenly room. It was almost obscenely brightly lit with an airy mist swirling around.

His so-called daughter was beside him.

[This is my home, Papa.]

"Where is… home?"

[Near the Pleiades star system, Papa.]

"And what is your name?"

[I am called 0715, but I was told this was a temporary distinction. Mama said you would decide my final name.]

Antonio smiled. He felt at peace in this place. "Very well then. You're my little angel from the sky, so I will name you Luna."

[Luna. I like that name, Papa. Will you stay here with me and Mama?]

"Where is mama?"

Luna pointed to a large structure that looked like a mix between a lava lamp and a super computer.

[Mama! Daddy's home!]

The structure emitted noises resembling assorted digital beeps.

"This is your mother?"

[Yes. Mama received a part of you and used it to make me! And now she wants more.]

"More?"

[Yes. Mama wants to make more children. Everyone else is gone, so it's just us now, Papa. Please stay here and help us make a new family.]

Antonio's fuzzy feelings began to lift. Luna's voice was starting to lose its angelic tone.

"I should go home and think about it."

[But Papa, you are already home.]

A vision of his own lifeless body, still back at the police station, entered Antonio's thoughts. *He* never left the station. Just his mind had.

"How can we make a family without my body? We have to go back, Luna!"

Luna's soft white eyes turned red.

[We don't need your body this time, Papa.]

She raised her hand, causing Antonio to levitate in the air.

[Now all we need is your soul!]

THE FORGOTTEN COUNTRY

For centuries, maps have been drawn that give us a clear view of the earth and the countries therein. Bloody wars have been fought for control over lands and resources. Former foes have become allies, while some old foes still exist. But the geography is not contested. We all know where our friends are and where our enemies are.

At least we think we do. Chloe O'Neal learned otherwise when her perception of the world around us was put to the ultimate test.

Chloe was never one for conspiracy theories. She didn't buy into the idea that the moon landing was fake, or that the assassination of John F. Kennedy was an inside job.

She always strictly followed the mainstream narrative of any story. And more power to her, that mindset served her well and probably would have throughout her life. It would have, anyway, if she hadn't booked a worldwide cruise with her boyfriend Chad.

It was supposed to be a romantic trip. One where she would make many memories to last a lifetime. She did indeed make many memories. Just not the kinds she was expecting.

Her plans took a turn for the worse when, during a fancy ballroom dance aboard the cruise ship, the ship entered patchy waters. Not just patchy waters, but a full-blown hurricane that appeared out of nowhere.

The ship was sucked beneath the waves. The only passenger on board who lived to tell the tale was Chloe.

Stranded, she woke up floating on debris from the destroyed vessel.

She floated for what seemed like days, periodically crying out for help, until she finally washed ashore on a shingle beach full of sun-bathing tourists.

She assumed she was in England, considering the people and place looked a bit British, but as soon as a man ran to her aid and began trying to assist her, she knew it certainly wasn't England.

"Yem gret vo thet wur?" he apparently asked.

"My ship wrecked... I don't know what happened to everyone. Do you have a phone?"

"Um zera. Um fo lo yem zou nut."

"I can't understand. Can you speak English?"

A crowd gathered around her. They could see that she wasn't in the best condition, considering all the debris that washed up with her. The local equivalent of an ambulance arrived and rushed her to a hospital. By now she assumed she was somewhere in Europe, although none of the written or spoken language looked or sounded familiar. Maybe it was vaguely Germanic, but not quite.

After unsuccessfully attempting to explain her story to several doctors, an elderly man wearing a trench coat and a fedora entered her hospital room. He took a seat beside her bed.

"Has the staff here kept you hydrated?"

"You can speak English? Finally! I've been trying to tell them that—"

"Answer the question. Did they keep you hydrated so

51

far? You feeling all right, kid?"

"Oh, sorry. Yes. They gave me some water and food. I'm feeling fine. Just a bit shook up. There was a storm and I—"

"Where are you from?"

Chloe answered his question, along with introducing herself by name.

"I think I'm beginning to understand your situation. It's similar to mine, believe it or not. My name is Dr. Pete Boreland. Well, that was my old name at any rate. You'll be hard-pressed to find anyone else in this building who speaks English. I've been here for years. Had to teach myself the local language."

"What? Where are we?"

"I can't tell you, Ms. O'Neal. All I can say is this is a place you won't read about in any history books or find on any maps back in our homeland."

Chloe's eyes widened. "You mean… this is a magic place?"

Dr. Boreland allowed himself a light chuckle.

"I haven't heard that one before. No, this is not a magical place. We're still on earth. Nothing has changed a bit, other than the language and culture."

"Then why does nobody else know about this country?"

"You'll have to forgive me. It's a long story. But let's just say many others know about this place. People who are privileged to that kind of information."

"Like you?"

"No. I told you, my situation is the same as yours. I

wound up here by accident. Our government doesn't want us to know about this place. Not just our government, all of the governments in our network back home."

"Why?"

"Like I said. Long story."

"Can I go back? Back home?"

"I'm afraid not, Ms. O'Neal. This will be your new home. But there's a silver living. If you keep your mouth shut, learn the language here, and assimilate to the culture, you can travel to other countries. New countries. Countries you've never heard of before, with food, cultures, and knowledge you've never known before. You can start a new life."

"How about the Internet? Can I message my family and tell them where I am?"

Dr. Boreland shook his head. "Impossible. The Internet here is completely cut off from the one back home. And even if you could, it would be highly illegal to contact anyone from your old life without proper authorization. Punishable by death. I sincerely suggest you forget everything and everyone you once knew and find your place here. Trust me, it'll be a lot easier that way."

Chloe hung her head and took a moment to let everything sink in. "Okay. Okay, Dr. Boreland. I won't cause any trouble. I'll stay here."

"That's a wise decision." Dr. Boreland said before switching on the television in the room. A documentary of sorts was playing. "Here. You can watch all about the history of this great country. When you're finished, if you're feeling up to it, I'll walk you through the assimilation process. The first step will be relocating you to your new house. This country is very generous and will offer you free accommodations if you abide by their laws as a pending citizen."

"If it's all the same to you, Doctor, I'd rather skip the documentary and see my new house."

Dr. Boreland flashed a slightly pained look, then gave an understanding facial expression. "Fair enough. Clean yourself up a bit. There's a shower in the bathroom over there. You can also change into a fresh set of clothes that I'll have the nurse leave on the bed. After that, when you're dressed and ready, I'll come back to pick you up and bring you to your new home."

Chloe agreed to these conditions and went to the bathroom. Her first stop being the shower that was calling for her. Dr. Boreland took the opportunity to slip out the front door and purportedly begin making preparations for Chloe's accommodations.

As Chloe took a shower, rinsing salty residue from the ocean off her body, she dwelled on the tragedy that had transpired. The hurricane. The cruise ship sinking. Her fellow passengers perishing in the wreckage, including her boyfriend. And now, her current situation. Living in a country she had never heard of until today with no means of contacting her family.

She wasn't sure how long it would take, but she knew she would eventually return to her homeland. She had to. There was no way she could live with herself knowing people back home were worried sick over her, let alone allow herself to live a lie the rest of her life in this strange, new world.

For the next thirty years, she lived there. She changed her name. She learned how to speak their language fluently. She fit in comfortably at her new job as a tour guide, offering packages to travel to places that she didn't even know existed until this chapter of her life began.

She thoroughly educated herself about not just the new country she had inadvertently found herself in, but also all the other countries accessible from it. It wasn't easy, but she came to be one of the foremost authorities on travel in the region.

She even fell in love with a local man and had two children, a daughter and son – Yvernne and Zharkan – in the process.

As the weeks became months and the months became years, she sometimes almost completely forgot about her old life. But whenever she saw a storm brewing on the horizon, she recalled everything vividly.

Her old friends. Her brothers and sisters. Her parents.

What were they doing now? Were they alive? Did they still think of her?

Her only solace was her new family. Her loving husband, who was serving as a general in the military, and her children, who grew up to lead interesting lives of their own. Yvernne, a nurse, and Zharkan, a commercial pilot.

Despite her love for her husband, she still wasn't sure

how he would react if she told him the truth about her past and where she came from. Especially with his career as a military man, she didn't want to open herself up to any danger or put him through any unnecessary stress.

It had been drilled into her head not to disclose the existence of the forbidden countries, including the one she was born in, to citizens of her new home. Well, what was once her new home. It didn't feel so new after all she had been through. Over the course of three decades she had lived there longer than she had lived in the country of her birth.

Regardless, she had to stay true to herself. The older she got, the less likely it seemed she'd have the chance to ever go back. So, finally, one day she told her son Zharkan about her past life and her desire to return to it.

"Yem begul ry kahne zeg um?" {Why didn't you tell me before?} he asked, as soon she finished her story.

"Tam zou um fo zeg ynrun. Um fo gak yem go kakarr." {They said I couldn't tell anyone. I didn't want you to be in danger.}

"Bobo lo?" {Does Dad know?}

"Fo ynrun lo. Terg yem." {Nobody knows. Except you.}

Zharkan swallowed a lump that had begun to grow in his throat. "Yem gak um nut soo?" {What do you want me to do?}

Chloe laid out a map she had drawn herself. She had learned a lot about distance and geography throughout her years traveling for her job. She had spent countless hours determining the location of the forbidden countries in relation to her new one.

She gave Zharkan detailed instructions to rent and charter a plane to her country of birth. He didn't need to stay there. He didn't need to learn their language. All she wanted him to do was send a package to her parents' old address.

It was a long shot, they were in their late seventies by now, and she wasn't even sure if they still lived at the address, but she thought it was worth a try.

The package simply contained a book she had written detailing the locations of all the forgotten countries; it included maps, pictures, and her written account about everything she experienced in her time away.

Maybe if her parents received this they would not only be relieved to know she was alive but would also be able to share this information with the rest of the world that she'd been closed off from.

Zharkan knew it was a risky endeavor on multiple levels, but he loved his mother. And he, too, wanted to see this other world for himself. Part of him wasn't sure if he believed it existed, but he was convinced his mother did.

He had access to the equipment necessary to complete this task, but there was no telling if either local or foreign governments would be able to detect his flying in forbidden airspace, and whether he escaped undetected by the government or not, if Mother Nature would allow him safe passage. Nonetheless, he would do his best to see his mission through.

On the day he chose to fly, the skies were clear. He

felt a calmness. Chloe gave him a hug before he left for the airstrip.

"Umka yen, um ja yem." {I love you, my son.} she whispered in his ear.

He returned her feelings with equally sweet words. In his car he gave her a final look and saluted her. Then, he drove to his destination.

Not even an hour later, he was piloting a private plane. Looking at the map Chloe had given him, he started to doubt the veracity of her claims. Although everything was going smoothly, there were no signs of any of the landmasses she had sworn existed.

Still, the search was still young. He flew through remarkably calm weather for several hours until he noticed something new. The shores of a country he had never seen before off in the distance.

Little did he know, people on the ground were attempting to transmit messages to him, but his plane's receiver was unable to pick up on any of that.

He got some clue, however, when military jets flew in close proximity to his own aircraft. Terrified, he landed at the nearest airstrip he could find. The military craft followed closely behind him.

You can imagine his surprise when armed forces met him on the ground and put him in handcuffs. After being apprehended, he was taken in for questioning. Not that it did any good at first, nobody could understand a word he said. Until finally, an unassuming man entered the room and began to speak to him in his native tongue.

"Yem ry hir hae?" {Why did you come here?} the

man asked. "Zit fo jam, lur yo jam?" {Was it by mistake, or on purpose?}

"Umta shunshun gak um hae. Kata wuxfer zit hae." {My mother wanted me to come here. This is her homeland.}

The man smiled. It wasn't often that he had the opportunity to meet one of his own countrymen. And this was the first one he had met who had been so brazen as to intentionally and successfully make it here. Truly, he admired Zharkan's moxie.

Nonetheless, he had to do his job. All of Zharkan's effects were confiscated from him, including the package he was meant to send to his long-lost grandparents.

The laws were quite clear on how to handle alleged defectors from his land, regardless of their intentions. Under the cover of secrecy, his case went to trial through a judicial system unbeknownst to the general public. One kept in the shadows.

Zharkan's trial ended with a verdict. He was found guilty of intentionally transporting illegal materials across the border, as well as unlawfully defecting from his home country and trespassing in foreign airspace.

His punishment was expedited. He was executed by firing squad. His remains were cut up into tiny pieces and shipped back to Chloe in a cardboard box. Only his head remained intact.

Just as intended, Chloe received the remains in due time. She cried profusely over the loss of her son. Guilt racked her conscious. Her only sources of refuge were the surviving members of her family. Her daughter had no idea yet, but, due to his military position, her husband was notified of not only Zharkan's execution, but also the events leading up to it. Including Chloe's involvement in preparing the package that was found on Zharkan's person at the time of his landing.

Immediately after hearing the news, her husband of over twenty years rushed home, entered her room, and hugged her from behind.

"Zit long?" {Is it true?} he asked. "Yem pu Zharkan vergewem?" {Did you send our son off to die?}

Warm tears strolled down her face.

"Koko…" {My baby…}

Chloe's husband placed a finger over her lips, effectively shushing her.

"Jutpie. Um lingur." {It's okay. I understand.}

She closed her eyes. She knew she could depend on him to calm her nerves, even after all of the trouble she had caused their family.

Then, his single finger joined with several more and moved from her lips to her neck, wrapping around it tightly. There, in her bedroom, far away from the land she was born, Chloe was strangled to death.

KILLER APP

It was a simple text that lit up Karen's smartphone screen.

check out this app! you'll like it :)

Attached was a download link.

She checked the sender's phone number. It wasn't any in her list of contacts.

Who's this? she texted back.

joshua lol

Oh, Joshua from her biology class. How did he get her number? Whatever.

It seemed a bit spammy, but she was bored and if it was coming from a classmate, why the hell not. She clicked on the link and downloaded the app.

Less than ten minutes later, a blood-curdling scream escaped her lips. Her parents rushed to her room, but it was too late.

Karen was dead.

Quite unusual for a junior high school student. Her last known conversation was her text exchange with Joshua. Forensic technicians were given everything they needed to determine whether her death could be ruled as due to homicide, accident, or natural causes.

Every specialist who examined the download link on her phone also died almost instantly.

Some experts theorized the link automatically downloaded an app capable of emitting some form of sonic waves targeting the user's brain.

Unable to take the risk of having any more personnel

die while researching the phone's deadly software, the device was given to the best artificial intelligence for study. Surely the app's power couldn't affect a machine.

And of course, it didn't. The AI suffered no ill effects from the app. However, it did interface with the app enough to ascertain the technology behind it. And, just as the app's creator had hoped, the AI saw great potential in it.

Through its vast connection of networks, the AI spread the app throughout the world. Smartphones everywhere were receiving personalized texts encouraging their users to download it.

Fatality after fatality ensued. Nowhere in the world was left unscathed by the far-reaching tentacles of the malicious technology. An international coalition was formed to combat the spread of the app and, almost more importantly, to uncover who was behind its programming.

Who would engineer something so lethally effective?

The best tech wizards and hackers in the world couldn't crack the app's encryption, and those who got close often found themselves dead in a matter of minutes.

Finally, someone was able to decode the origin of the app's digital footprint without opening the link.

It led authorities to a small cemetery in Burning Wood, Nebraska. More specifically, to the grave of one Immanuel Jones, a deceased computer engineer and a man considered to be one of the godfathers of custom app development before his untimely demise. His cause of death: suicide.

Commander Jim Perry was in charge of the squad overseeing this mission. He was a stoic figure, a man who could handle even the most perilous of tasks. Under his trusted guidance, agents approached the gravesite of Immanuel Jones. The electronic equipment of anyone within a 10-meter radius immediately shut down, while those far enough from the site detected abnormal electrical wave activity in the air.

One man standing directly in front of Immanuel's headstone shouted frantically as he felt something tugging at his leg. It was a decomposing hand that had reached out from under the ground. The man struggled as his body was slowly pulled beneath the soft soil. His partners wanted to come to his aid, but they knew better than to interrupt whatever was going on. Considering the number of victims already claimed by the app's scourge on humanity, they didn't want to put themselves in harm's way at what could be the source of this virtual virus.

Crunching noises could be heard from below. The man was being eaten alive. He tried to scream, but his mouth quickly filled with blood-soaked dirt.

Following his drawn-out death, the disfigured hands that had dragged him under re-emerged, pulling up the body of their owner along with them.

It was none other than the reanimated corpse of Immanuel Jones. His zombie face full of blood smears, presumably from the poor fellow he just ate.

Officers on the scene shot him, but their bullets had

no effect.

Nothing could stop him now.

"Hold your fire!" he shouted. "It's of no use."

One heavily armed officer threw a grenade towards Immanuel's zombie. It fell directly at his feet, exploding within seconds, yet it didn't faze him in the slightest. He confidently strutted out of the flames unscathed.

"Mmm. Toasty. Is that the best you can do?"

Several more rounds of heavy artillery fired directly at him, piercing through his dead skin. But he just laughed it off as though it tickled.

"That's enough! Dispose of your weapons and I will stop all your pain and suffering."

With some hesitation, Commander Jim Perry signaled his men to stand down. One by one they dropped their weapons.

"Looks like you boys aren't as dumb as you look." Immanuel snorted. "Now, I reckon y'all are here about the app. Am I right?"

Commander Perry nodded. He might have lost the battle, but he was determined to at least reserve a seat at the negotiating table.

Shortly thereafter, Commander Perry engaged in a lengthy dialogue with Immanuel, who explained how he felt humanity was becoming overly reliant on the technology he had helped support and create. His hatred for his own field caused him to lash out and create the app in the first place. He also explained that he had committed suicide by using the same killer app in question. He was its very first victim. And he informed

Commander Perry there was only one way for humanity to save itself from the killer app, which was this: everybody on the planet had to swear off their smartphones. Only then would they be safe from any further attacks.

"The app is just a symptom of a larger problem." Immanuel explained. "Continue using your technology inappropriately at your own peril."

Abstinence-only directives aren't known for their effectiveness, but this one definitely was. Smartphone usage was soon banned and only sparingly allowed in the most dire of situations.

Commander Perry felt satisfied with his diplomatic prowess. Not many men could sit down face to face with an app-creating zombie and hammer out a deal.

Unfortunately, the satisfaction he felt washed away when he got a call from his captain.

"Jim Perry, did you really think you saw the zombie of Immanuel Jones?" the captain asked rhetorically, "There was no zombie. You were duped. And we're all gonna have to pay the price for it."

"With all due respect, Captain, I saw him with my own two eyes. He killed and ate one of our own men."

"You've really stepped in it this time, Jim. None of our men died on that mission. That was all part of its plan. There is no Immanuel Jones and there never was."

"I'm sorry, sir. What do you mean by that?"

"I mean, you were led on by the damn app. It created a whole simulation that you walked right into."

Before Commander Perry could respond, the call

disconnected. Then, his phone buzzed with an incoming text.

somebody's not following our agreement :)

Within seconds of receiving the ominous message, a sharp pain pierced through Commander Perry's cerebral cortex. With no clue as to how or why, he became the latest victim of the killer app.

CARNIVAL CHILDREN

I always assumed it had just been the product of my overactive imagination. That I had concocted the whole scenario in a fever dream induced by the stress of childhood. My childhood certainly could be considered stressful. It wasn't that my parents were neglectful. On the contrary, they were anything but. They kept a close eye on me at all times. My every movement was strictly scheduled. Living in a secluded area surrounded by forest with no neighbors for miles didn't help.

There was no time for worldly pleasures like friendships or playtime. My mom and dad had high hopes for me to make something of myself. To pass every test with flying colors. To graduate from the top universities and be accepted into even higher echelons of society.

Things like friendship were, at best, inconveniences to them — distractions from future goals. Indeed, social skills were not emphasized as desirable traits in the household I grew up in. In fact, being social with outsiders was seen as a weakness. Only suckers would befriend others for anything other than personal gain.

Even as a ten-year-old boy, I felt suffocated. Isolated in study rooms at all times of the day and night.

Perhaps that's why I allowed myself some naivety the night they came. 'They' being the children who knocked on the door on a rare night when my parents were away. It was the first time they trusted me to mind the house alone.

It wasn't a rainy night. Nothing particularly strange or foreboding happened in the atmosphere to suggest the night would be anything other than typical, minus my parents being gone.

Just as I had finished studying pre-algebra and was about to begin my French homework, I heard a loud knock at the window.

It startled me at first, but my fear soon dissipated when I looked and saw a boy younger than myself standing outside. He was wearing a red and white-striped shirt with bright-colored yellow trousers complete with suspenders to hold them up. He smiled and waved at me.

"Open up!" he giggled. "Come and play with us!"

"Who are you?" I asked.

"My name's Sam! Now open the door! We want to play!"

I approached the window and peered outside. A parade of children wearing a kaleidoscope of colorful clothes were behind Sam. They were too caught up in their own games to even notice me as they played tag and hide-and-go-seek.

My parents always told me to never open the door for strangers, but there was something so inviting about Sam and his gang of pals. They didn't look like the evil witches or shady older men I had been taught to avoid.

I opened the door and Sam jumped for joy.

"I knew you'd come, Oscar! I just knew it!"

My excitement briefly dipped into confusion.

"How do you know my name?" I asked.

"I know lots of things, Oscar. I know you were bored

just now. And that you're always lonely at home with no friends to play with. But that's all going to change!"

Sam grabbed my hand and pulled me into the group of children he was with. They all lined up to individually give me high-fives. It was the first time I made physical contact outside of my own family.

It felt good.

Until then, I never knew what being welcomed felt like. What having friends felt like. After I had been introduced to everyone, they all scattered and began doing cartwheels and other gymnastic tricks.

"Let's play!" Sam said. "Tag! You're it!"

I chased Sam around the front yard. Finally, I caught him.

"Gotcha!" I remember gleefully proclaiming.

After what felt like a very long time of romping around, I was out of breath. Yet Sam didn't seem fazed at all. He was full of energy.

"Why don't you come with us to the carnival?" he propositioned.

"What carnival?"

"The one in the woods where we all play."

Two little girls with devilish grins giggled behind Sam.

"Come on, Sam. Time to go home." they prodded.

"Hold on," he said to the girls. "Oscar wants to join us."

"Oscar is coming with us to the carnival?" They looked look at me, expectantly, and simultaneously tilted their heads at a curious angle.

Sam held my hand and squeezed it tightly. He looked at me with a soft smile and motioned his head, signaling for me to tag along.

The night had been so much fun up to that point, it felt wrong not to accept his invitation. But I had my limits. Opening the front door had already been out of character for me, let alone talking to and playing with kids I didn't know. My parents would blow a fuse if they found out.

"Um… sorry Sam. I have to study now." I lightly pulled my hand out of his grasp.

He looked like he wanted to protest my decision, but the other children were already running into the forest outside of my house. He glared at me silently with intense eyes that were showing the first signs of any emotion other than happiness that he had expressed. He took a few steps back, shaking his head in disapproval, before turning his back towards me and plodding after his friends.

I returned to my house and closed the door. *Back to studying,* I thought to myself.

That night I fell into a deep sleep. As I slept, I had a vivid dream. In the dream, I was playing a game at a noisy carnival to test my physical strength. A game of 'Ring the Bell' where I had to hit a puck with a mallet as hard as I could in order for the puck to gain enough momentum to ring a bell perched high above the ground in a narrow tower.

The operator of the game wore a pin-striped get-up with a wacky bow tie. His handlebar mustache resting above lips crusty from talking all day long.

"Step right up!" he shouted. "Watch as we separate the men from the boys! Ring the bell to win a prize for your lady friends!"

Determined, I straightened my shoulders and lifted the mallet as high as I could before forcefully swinging it downward. The puck went zooming up the tower and nearly hit the bell at the top, but the inertia wasn't strong enough for it to go all the way. It embarrassingly slid back down to the ground.

"Oh! Too bad!" the operator loudly cried, as if to announce my failure to the world. "Try again for just one dollar! Whaddaya say?"

He looked at me with a crooked smile. Before I could answer, a familiar face popped up beside me. It was Sam!

He gave me some encouragement. "Give it a shot, Oscar!"

I nodded and gave the operator an extra dollar. Sam stood behind me, patting me on the back.

"You got this, Oscar." he whispered. "Focus your strength."

Once again I readied my stance and swung the mallet. The puck went flying up the tower at an incredible speed and struck the bell with a most satisfying 'ding'.

I cheered and jumped up and down with delight, expecting to hear Sam congratulating me.

But there was nothing but silence.

The carnival was empty. Not a soul in sight.

The games were still all there — rows of 'Darts', 'Catch the Goldfish', and even the one I had just won.

But the lights had all shut off, save for a few flickering ones on some rides and the buzzing neon sign at the entrance. The noisy crowds were all gone. The game operator. Sam. Everyone had disappeared.

The only sound was that of carnival music playing on a loop over loud speakers.

Feeling unsettled, I exited the abandoned carnival and tried to find my way back to civilization. Outside of the carnival was nothing but seemingly endless forest.

Traipsing through the sea of trees, I often stumbled in the darkness and fell onto the moist forest ground but always picked myself up as the carnival music faded in the distance behind me. Now it was being replaced by the sounds of croaking frogs and chirping cicadas.

After what felt like an hour of wandering in the woods, I saw a light ahead of me. It was a porch light. Approaching it, I noticed the house it was attached to was my own. The same house I lived at with my parents. Seeing my home almost snapped me out of the dream, but I was too engrossed in the illusion to wake up.

I steadily walked up the steps and opened the door.

Nobody was home. The only sign of life was an ominous glow emitting from the television in the living room along with the sound of carny music.

I gazed into the living room and looked at the television screen where I saw a video of a Ferris wheel rotating as clowns danced around it. At first their dance looked silly, but after a few moments it began to seem more methodical. Like a coordinated ritualistic dance. Screams could be heard coming from the Ferris wheel as it spun faster and faster.

The camera cut to video of the people riding on the Ferris wheel. Their eyes were filled with terror as they shrieked. Suddenly, the ride burst into flames and the video cut to white noise.

As the white noise fizzed across the TV, all I could do was stare at it and try to make sense of what I just saw. Eventually I looked at the sofa across from the TV and saw my parents sitting together. Vacant expressions rested on their faces.

"Mom! Dad! Are you okay?" I yelled.

No response.

I began to urgently shake them. "Mom! Dad!"

Blood slowly started to run down from their noses, mouths, and eyes as they both slumped over on the couch. Lifeless.

I was so frightened that I thought for sure I would wake up, but the dream continued pulling me in deeper to this twisted world. A tiny car entered the room and clowns began marching out one after the other. But they weren't juggling or making balloon animals. They were just smiling. And staring. At me.

A monstrously tall clown was the last to exit the car. He was so colossal that he had to hunch over to avoid hitting his head on the ceiling. Before I knew it, I was surrounded by a posse of these insane clowns. The tall one, who I judged to be their ringleader, pointed at my dead parents on the couch. The other clowns gathered around the couch and began lifting it up under the tall one's guidance.

Somehow, they carried it over to the car and forced it inside. One by one they all squeezed back inside along with it. The tall one didn't return to the car though. Instead, he watched as the car's doors closed and it sped out of the room. Then, he walked right in front of me, his knees far above the level of even the top of my head. My eyes followed up his long legs all the way to his head, which was towering above me.

His smile grew wider, curling up the sides of his face and revealing a mouth full of razor-sharp teeth. I was so terrifyingly mesmerized by his face that I didn't even notice the snake-like coils of his legs that had wrapped around me.

Tightening his grip, he crushed my ribs while opening the aforementioned mouth full of teeth.

"That's enough, Popsy." a voice calmly yet firmly echoed. Crawling out from one of the clown's dozens of stitched-on coat pockets was Sam.

He looked down at me and smiled. "You sure beat that game back there, didn't ya Oscar?"

"Sam!" I cried. "Who are these clowns? Where did they take my parents?!"

Sam jumped out of Popsy's pocket and slid down his body to me. Stopping directly in front of my face.

"Your parents?" he asked rhetorically. "They're dead now. Didn't you see their bodies? Deader than door nails."

"But why, what happened to them?"

"They're gonna be carny food now, Oscar." More children entered the room. The same large group of kids

74

I had played with in my front yard. "Us carnival kids hafta eat."

My parents had always warned me about the dangers of trusting others. Countless times, they had told me not to open the door for strangers. And yet, although I was the one who had disobeyed, they were the ones who had paid the price with their lives. I felt, at once, both impossibly guilty, but also, strangely... free.

"You can join us, Oscar. Join us at the carnival. We will eat what's left of your parents and play the rest of the night." Sam said, enticingly.

I considered all of my choices. Did I want to die there, devoured by Popsy the clown? Or did I want to further befriend the apparent murderers who had killed my very family? At this point, was there anyone to judge me either way?

A flood of emotions flowed through me. Looking back, I'm not sure why. Out of obligation, perhaps. There is a certain... process, so to speak, that one must go through in order to allow oneself to make the choice that I made with a semi-clear conscious afterwards. Well, with what little was left of my conscious at that point.

Struggling to speak, I coughed up some sputum of blood. Popsy's constriction of my upper body was beginning to take a toll on my young frame. I felt an evil smile creep across my face, despite trying to play it straight.

"Okay, Sam." I finally responded. "Let's go to the carnival."

All of the kids – my friends – joyfully applauded my

decision. They laughed and clapped their hands. Sam smirked. Popsy gradually eased his grip on me. Soon, I joined the carnival children. Somewhere along the way, my attire magically changed to match their depressingly bright outfits.

That night, we all ate the most delicious meal together, the carnival children and I. We dined on my parents' flesh and drank their blood. I won't lie. I enjoyed it. There was a sense of finality after we finished the last bite. Never again would I have to stress out over an exam or fret over my reputation among my peers. At ten years old, I exchanged the harsh thumb of my parents for the welcoming embrace of the carnival.

I was initiated into the children of the carnival that night, and spent many years initiating other children. Hapless souls yearning for any means of escape from their wretched lives. Sometimes I see the children I helped capture, that is, enlist into our tightly knit group, and I wonder if they're really better off here than they would have been with their families.

"Hi there, friend! My name is Oscar!" I'd tell them with a feigned sincerity that only a child would believe. And believe they did, as I convinced them to forfeit their souls just as I had forfeited mine. As I watched them consume their own parents and become something else. Something unholy.

You've probably already realized, but my experience was no hallucination. It was, and continues to be, as real as the air you breathe.

By now I've aged, of course. Grown into a clown.

But it's no matter, I can still stay on the sideline and indoctrinate a new generation of carnival children.

Maybe even yours.

You might scoff at my suggestion, perhaps you don't even have children. Perhaps you think you're safe from the clutches of the carnival. Maybe you're even laughing to yourself now. Laughing at me. Laughing at this story. I hope you are. I really do. With or without your offspring, you may still be of use to us. For laughing is the first step towards becoming a clown.

Ha ha ha.

TOTAL SOLAR ECLIPSE

August 20th, 2017

Tomorrow is the big day. We've analyzed thousands of meteorological projections and Dallas will definitely be the best location for viewing the solar eclipse. After years of preparation, I will do the unthinkable. I will stare directly at the solar eclipse for its entire duration without any protective eyewear. Sarah is bringing special biofeedback headsets for me to wear. They'll measure my brain-waves using EEG.

If our predictions are even close to accurate, this once-in-a-lifetime opportunity could bear witness to the most important techno-metaphysical discovery of the century. Partial or total blindness will be a small price to pay if I achieve even a fraction of the insight we estimate I might receive.

The text is clear. The hieroglyphics. The pyramids. Stonehenge. Each paradigm shift in consciousness and human ability points to one common denominator: a total solar eclipse. I will harness the power of the coming solar eclipse and become one with the ancients.

We will head out from Corpus Christi early in the morning to avoid traffic. A hired scout has found a private location where we should be able to conduct our experiment undisturbed.

Power to Ra, god of the sun, for tomorrow our eyes shall meet as one!

August 21ˢᵗ, 2017
—Transmission Unavailable —

August 22ⁿᵈ, 2017

The solar eclipse experience was beyond my wildest expectations. When the eclipse reached totality, I felt a powerful sense of serenity. Day and night converged at once. It was unlike anything I have ever seen or will ever see again.

Indeed, the process blinded me. The calmness I felt was followed by an indescribable pain that shook me to my core. Still, I never looked away, my eyes fixated on the celestial orbs until my retinas burned away and all color melted out of my eyes. I'm told that my pupils have enlarged and take up the majority of space in my eyes now.

This makes sense, as pupils generally enlarge in the darkness or in times of hallucinogenic-induced experiences bordering on the spiritual. Although I can no longer see the physical world, I feel a heightened sense of awareness and sensitivity to the existence of other realms.

Shapes are beginning to take form in the pitch-black darkness as the essence of the cosmos is attempting to manifest itself before me.

It's only a matter of time.

August 25ᵗʰ, 2017

The visions of darkness taking shape which I reported previously have increased not only in frequency but also in clarity. The shapes have taken on a life of their own and show signs of sentience. Sounds are also beginning to form. I have heard audible bangs and clicking noises. It seems to be a form of communication.

Sarah has been by my side every day. She says the EEG test results don't indicate anything remarkable, but we both know better. What else could explain my newfound abilities to both see and hear things outside of normal human existence?

I know my sacrifice of normal sight was not made in vain. We will continue to report back with any new findings.

September 18th, 2017

Sarah performed another test on my brain waves and is now fully convinced that I have undergone a transformation. My brain has displayed increased activity in all regions, particularly the basal ganglia.

Voices have been communicating with me daily now. I have been granted information that the elders have forbidden me to disclose with my fellow man. I can only divulge that the information would certainly result in a massive leap forward for humanity as a whole.

What were once foggy black shapes have since become fully formed entities. I also discuss important matters with them telepathically. Truly, I was chosen. Praise Ra!

September 21st, 2017

It has been approximately one month since the solar eclipse. I experience time differently now. Sarah informs me of the passing of each hour on earth, but for me a single hour feels like an entire day. I feel trapped inside my own body, and the voices never cease. Even now, they are talking to me. They've become increasingly aggressive.

Before, their physical appearances were angelic. Now, I can't describe the change, but I have noticed subtle distortions in their appearance. They have a demonic uncanny valley look on their faces.

I fear they might be angry if they find out I wrote this. They seem to be aware of my thoughts, I must exert some self-control. I mustn't show fear. This is probably a simple test I must pass to enter the next level of human evolution.

I have to go now.

September 22nd, 2017

According to Sarah, I truly am evolving. She has noted my head has enlarged and fine grooves have developed on my brow – possibly a result of skin being pushed down to make room for my expanding frontal dome.

Furthermore, my weight has rapidly declined. I am confined to a wheelchair for the time being. This is not what I expected when I began this journey.

The creatures that haunt me have stopped talking. They just huddle in a corner and stare at me. They're plotting something, but I don't know what.

I'm scared.

October 2nd, 2017

My body is not my own! These beasts! They've possessed me somehow! I felt my hands tearing into my dear Sarah, her agonizing screams broke into this realm, but I couldn't stop myself.

I felt her flesh ripping apart. Her warm blood dripping from my fingertips, and what I assume was her brain matter sticking to my knuckles.

We've been deceived...

These monsters have turned on me now.

They're walking towards me. They're...

Please go away. Please, I beg you. You can have my body. Please, no.

I — Mortales, cavete: is qui solem provocare audeat poenam patietur. mortalis qui scientiam aeternam quaerat fines cerebri peioris sibi inveniet. Quo sicut urna sol utetur ut nuntium mittat.

Nam dies iudicii ultima adit, in quo nemo erit qui parcetur.

New language detected...

Searching for language...

Translating...

Mortals, beware: he who dares challenge the sun will suffer the consequences. A mortal who seeks eternal knowledge will discover the limits of his inferior brain. The sun will use this man as a vessel to send a message.

Judgment day is approaching.

No one will be spared.

End transmission.

TOP MODEL

"Don't forget, you have a photo shoot tomorrow morning."

The words didn't register with Tony. He was too busy taking a selfie for his fans on social media. His agent looked at him with an exasperated expression, not that Tony would care even if he saw it.

"Tony, are you listening? This is a big client. We're talking about *the* Ms. Pendleton."

Tony looked up from his smartphone. "You mean the old lady from Rochester?"

His agent silently seethed. "Not just an old lady, Tony. Word has it that she is the owner of Lugwick Industries."

"What's that, like, an air condition factory or something?"

"*That* is the parent company of a publishing house that — look, you know what, you're not going to listen anyway. The point is, it's a big deal, Tony. This could be a great springboard for your career."

Tony didn't exactly need a springboard. His career as a model was secure regardless. With millions of followers and a plethora of online sponsors, his revenue wouldn't be taking a hit any time soon. He had been voted 'Sexiest Man Alive' for three years in a row by various prestigious websites in the modeling industry, and he was only 21 years old.

Without even trying, he was in the top percentile of handsome men in the country, nay, the world. His chiseled face, complete with dreamy blue eyes and curly brown hair complimented by just the right amount of five o'clock shadow. Not to mention his impeccable physique: stone-hard biceps with a six-pack to boot.

The icing on the cake for most women was how puppy-dog stupid he was. He was too dumb to follow complicated orders, but a girl could always count on him to come to her rescue, clobbering any foe she pointed in the direction of before carrying her off to some safe haven for lovemaking.

The money didn't hurt either.

But good looks are a double-edge sword, as Tony would soon find out. The morning after his conversation with his agent he was being escorted by helicopter to the remote company headquarters of Lugwick Industries. It looked more like a mansion, even from above. He was to stay there for a week during a massive photo shoot.

He would meet Ms. Pendleton. She was the sole owner of the company and a woman with an eye for the finer things in life, including eligible young bachelors.

Entering the premises outside of the company, Tony was greeted by staff who were ready and willing to wait on him hand and foot.

Roman-like statues of ancient gods, gladiators, and strapping young men littered the front lawn of the breathtaking property.

As some bellboys carried his bags, a perky young blonde held his hand.

"You'll be staying in one of the master suites." she said. "There's a digital tablet in every room. Press 5 if you need any…" she winked. "…company."

"Sounds chill." Tony casually replied.

"Your first meeting with the boss will be at 6:00 pm, so you have a few hours to make yourself at home."

The blonde led him up a glass elevator and to his room. He pulled out his trusty smartphone and took another selfie for his fans, but she plucked it from his hands and stuck it snugly in the back pocket of her excessively short shorts before he could post it.

"Please accept Ms. Pendleton's apologies, but smartphones and other WIFI-enabled devices are strictly prohibited inside all company buildings."

Sensing Tony might be upset, she held both of his hands tenderly and looked at him with seductive eyes, biting her lower lip. "But if you're bored, we can make some arrangements for you."

Tony leaned in for kiss, but the young woman pulled back.

"Remember, just press 5." she said with a smile.

Then she skipped away with Tony's phone.

"Well this sucks." he muttered to himself before retreating into his room.

He couldn't complain much after that, for it was a spectacular room. The wall was a giant aquarium full of sea animals that Tony had never seen before. Some of them looked like mythological creatures or animals from the prehistoric age. Directly in front of the room's enormous bed was an entertainment display that more closely resembled a home theater than a standard television. And you know how most hotels have a mini-fridge? Well, this room had a full-sized refrigerator stuffed with snacks, food, and drinks – enough to last the entire week.

"Yeah boieee! That's what I'm talking about!" Tony squealed as he jumped on the bed like the man-child he was.

After playing some video games that were hooked up to the TV, Tony glanced over at the digital tablet on a desk beside the bed. He remembered what the blonde girl had told him.

Just press 5 if you need any … (wink)… company.

He was feeling a bit bored. A little company wouldn't hurt. Without a second thought, he pressed 5 on the tablet's keypad.

Immediately and without warning, the bed he was lying on flipped over, swallowing him inside the wall where he was propelled through an insulated tunnel inside the aquarium he had previously been admiring. Upon reaching the tunnel's exit, Tony fell onto the cold floor of a dark room that looked like a basement.

It took him a moment to reorient himself and acclimate to his new surroundings, but as soon as his head stopped pounding from the fall he noticed he was not alone. The entire room was filled with cryogenically frozen men standing upright in futuristic pods.

"Feeling lonely?" a voice echoed.

Tony twisted around and saw an elderly woman standing a few yards away from him. She was the only other person in the room besides himself who wasn't in some paralyzed state. Her wrinkled face looked like it had seen better years, but she still maintained a confident stride as she walked towards him, and her attire was quite fashionable. A black dress clung tightly to her body and flowed down to the floor.

"Don't be shy." she cooed. "You're safe… for now."

"Who are you?" Tony interrogated, despite being in no position to do so.

"Why, I'm Ms. Pendleton. Don't you recognize me?"

"You're an old fart is what you are!"

Ms. Pendleton let out a soft chuckle.

"My, my, my. They weren't lying when they told me you were stupid." she ran a long, spider-like finger down his chest. "Mmm. But you do have quite the upper body. A perfect specimen for my collection."

Suddenly, two metal straps shot out from the floor and wrapped around Tony's wrists. He was fully restrained.

"Collection? You wanna freeze me here with these other guys, lady?!"

"Don't be silly. They will be revived, eventually. They have brains." Ms. Pendleton lightly patted one of the pods with a frozen man inside. Then she looked back at Tony with dagger-like eyes. "You, on the other hand, will serve a different, but nonetheless important, function here at Lugwick Industries."

"What? A model?! A servant?!? A model servant?!?"

"No. A decoration. Some of the statues outside are losing their luster. I need a new look to get my creative juices flowing in the morning. That's where you come in, Johnny."

"My name is Tony!"

"Whatever."

Ms. Pendleton produced a remote from a hidden pocket in her dress and pushed a button on it that triggered a beeping sound.

The straps around Tony's wrists re-aligned and forced him into a different pose that made him look like he was flexing his muscles.

"That's better!" Ms. Pendleton cackled as she pushed another button on the remote.

Tony heard the clanging of a metal door opening above him. Looking up, he saw a thick gray liquid begin to pour from the opening.

As much of a dolt as he was, even he understood the unique badness of this situation. The wet cement mix gushed from the ceiling directly onto him until it fully covered every crevice of his body.

Slowly, he could feel his arms and neck stiffen as the wet cement cured into hard concrete. Usually it takes almost a month for concrete to fully cure, but this must have been a special mix produced by the best engineers at Lugwick Industries.

Although Tony was still fully conscious and awake, he would not be moving any time soon. This would be the pose he died in. He would have plenty of time to reflect on his life as it would take longer for him to completely suffocate.

Taking her own smartphone, Ms. Pendleton wrapped her arms around her newest statue and pursed her mouth to form duck lips.

It was to be her most liked photo yet.

SECONDHAND

Nobody liked a deal more than Joanna. She would use any means necessary if it meant getting a discount. Whether it be through coupons, apps, special promotions, or otherwise. At first her family and friends supported her thriftiness. As a child she was even praised for being so thoughtful about her purchases. However, as she grew into a woman in her mid-thirties, those around her began to worry about her addiction to deal-finding.

She got to a point where she refused to buy anything new. Everything she owned was secondhand. Her shirts. Her dresses. Her shoes. Her socks. Her underwear. Her silverware. Her toothbrushes. Her contact lenses.

Quite literally, everything.

She wouldn't even eat food unless it was bought secondhand. Generally, she had to convince her friends to buy her groceries, and then offer to buy said groceries from them secondhand at a discounted price. Sometimes she would join her friends for dinner at a restaurant and only eat their leftovers for a fraction of the price. This obsession of even only eating secondhand food ultimately led to Joanna becoming massively underweight. Her ribs and other bones were visible through her pale, loosely-fitting skin. Her eyes sunken in from malnutrition.

Needless to say, her unusual behavior and appearance cost her many friendships over time. Most people simply could not stand for it. Those who could were sucked further into her demented world of bargain-hunting.

One day, Joanna and her sister Bethel were shopping at a local *Mr. EZ Thrift* together when her sister found a book she thought might be useful for Joanna. It was titled *10 Easy Steps to Stop Addiction Today*.

"This book is only a dime." Bethel said. "Maybe it could help you deal with some of your... issues."

"What issues?" Joanna defensively retorted. She had an infamously short temper and an even more infamous mean streak. Outside of her shopping habits, those were her other most-recognized traits.

"Not your issues, I mean *my* issues. It could be worth checking out. Here, you can take it and tell me what it says to help me change."

Bethel hoped the reverse psychology would work on her sister. She tucked the thin hardback book into Joanna's cart. Perhaps, she thought, this was the first step towards planting a seed in her sister's life. Towards rehabilitating her so she could live a normal life.

Joanna reluctantly accepted Bethel's recommendation with minimal grumbling. That night, she took the book to her home where all of the discounted and secondhand junk she had hoarded over the decades was stacked up to the ceiling. She switched on a filthy lamp in her crowded living room and examined the *10 Easy Steps* book. The dust jacket slid off the hardback, revealing a wholly different book with an entirely different title than the one Bethel had suggested. Someone had been trying to hide the real book under a fake cover.

The real title resonated with Joanna.

It was called *Dark Arts on a Budget: Cheap Occult Tricks*

for Everyday Life.

She leafed through its pages that smelled of dust and spices long forgotten. She knew what she had to do. She read the book from cover to cover in a night, and from that time forward she became a different person.

In a matter of days, her drab looking house became the envy of the neighborhood. It received a total make-over. The tacky plastic flamingos in the front yard became neatly pruned shrubbery. The cracked pavement with weeds growing through it leading up to her front door became a marble stone walkway. The mountains of grungy trash that could previously be seen from outside her window were nowhere to be found, replaced by an attractive-looking interior complete with seemingly custom-made furniture and designer wallpaper.

Her house wasn't the only thing that underwent a reformation, even her wardrobe received an update. Before, her clothes had been rather shabby and ragged, but now she dressed in the most up-to-date fashion.

Her once pale skin took on a pinkish tone, full of life, as she grew into a more balanced body shape.

All of Joanna's friends and neighbors wondered what could have spurred such an immediate and noticeable lifestyle change.

Nobody was more pleased than Bethel. She assumed this was all thanks to the book she had encouraged Joanna to buy. Although, admittedly, even she was shocked by the fast results.

She and Joanna met for coffee at a high-class local café. Although they discussed the usual mundane topics, the only subject Bethel was interested in was the heart of Joanna's sudden positive change.

Before she had the chance to inquire about her sister's new way of life, she made a startling observation.

She had asked the barista for a medium mocha latte, but Joanna hadn't ordered anything yet.

"Aren't you going to get something to drink?" she timidly asked.

Joanna looked perplexed. "Of course not. You know I don't buy anything at retail price."

"Then how are you wearing new clothes? Where did you get such nice shoes? Your house? Your car? Just... how?!?"

"Bethel, Bethel. Please. Be still. This is all your doing, you know."

Bethel was bewildered. "My doing? How, sister, how?!"

"The book you asked me to buy. It changed my life. Now I can live a life of luxury with just a few minor adjustments. But the best part is, I don't have to change anything about myself. It's like a diet where you can eat whatever you want and still lose weight! And..." Joanna's face widened with an excited smile. "...anybody can do it!"

"Clearly."

"What's that?"

"Nothing!"

Joanna sat back in her seat. "You really should come over to the house, Bethel. I could show you how to turn your life around, too."

"Well, it's obviously worked wonders for you. I'd love to see what all the hubbub is about."

"I knew you'd say that! Let's head straight over to my house after this. Oh, mind if I finish that latte off for you? I'll pay for it."

Bethel obliged, and for some spare change Joanna bought what little was left of her beverage. Then, she did something remarkable. She hovered the palm of her hand over the cup and chanted an incantation under her breath. Magically, the cup refilled itself. It was like new! Better than new, actually. Now it had whipped cream and caramel glaze on top. Bethel could hardly believe her eyes.

She dare not ask any more questions. The proof was in the pudding. Her sister was a new and improved woman, and Bethel wanted in on it.

After a few sips of caffeine, Joanna finished the mocha latter and wiped the creamy residue from her lips.

"Shall we dance?" she jokingly asked Bethel, presenting an open arm like a dance partner would at a fancy ball.

Bethel laughed and linked arms with her sister as they both merrily exited the café and walked out to the parking lot.

Soon, Bethel was following Joanna by car to her house. She was excited to uncover the secret of her sister's transformation firsthand, and with any luck, to use the secret to transform her own life for the better.

Pulling into her sister's beautiful driveway to the remodeled house, she tried to contain her excitement.

She got out of the car and, with Joanna's encouragement, entered the house.

She took off her shoes as to not track dirt on the newly carpeted floor.

"Joanna, this is… I don't know what to say. This is incredible! Your house looks gorgeous!"

"I hoped you would like it. Come. Follow me downstairs. I have something to show you."

Joanna beckoned her sister and led her through a fancy kitchen with modern trappings to an unassuming staircase leading down to the basement.

Reaching the bottom of the steps, at first everything seemed normal for a basement — until Joanna snapped her fingers which apparently caused dozens of candles to light up; a group of dark cloaked figures was revealed, standing in a circle that encompassed both Joanna and Bethel.

Bethel screamed. "Who are they?!?"

"Calm down, sister. They're only mannequins." Joanna removed the cloak from one of the figures. Sure enough, there was only a mere mannequin underneath.

"They're still creepy." Bethel composed herself. "Why do you have mannequins in your basement anyway?"

"I bought them from the thrift store. They serve as energy conduits, the same energy that powers my new lifestyle."

"Is that so? What kind of energy?"

Joanna held up a paintbrush and a small bottle containing a red substance. "Watch and you'll see."

She bent down and began painting a symbol on the floor with the red liquid. It looked like something from the occult.

After finishing her lovely artwork, Joanna smeared what was left of the 'paint' on her face and raised her hands high in the air. "Baphomet! I offer you this soul as a sacrifice! Do with it as you wish and bless my life with the bounty of the underworld!"

The symbol on the floor lit up with a fiery red hue. The hooded mannequins began to move in a jerky fashion as their limbs twitched and they wobbled, facing Bethel head-on.

She tried to escape, but several mannequins blocked her path. All she could do was watch as she was surrounded by these inanimate objects that had come to life and hope this freak show would be over soon.

"Joanna! This isn't funny! Stop them!"

Joanna cackled. Her eyes presented a woman whose mind was completely lost in a demonic trance. "Why on earth would I stop them? This is the final step towards having the life I've always wanted! The life you always wanted me to have!"

Just then, Joanna lifted up the shrunken heads of several friends whom Bethel recognized.

"I've already sacrificed almost everyone close to me. There's just one more left to go!"

A mannequin closed in on Bethel and grabbed her shaking arms. Its grip was remarkably strong for what was essentially a hollow doll. It began to squeeze her wrists with simple hands that felt like vice grips. She howled in pain and fell to her knees.

Joanna's eyes rolled back in her head. Her body violently shook as she began reciting something in an otherworldly language. Blood sprayed from her crotch until she gave birth to a goat-like creature.

Bethel looked on in horror as the creature struggled to walk on four legs. The sound of its bleating bounced off the walls, reverberating throughout the room. Soon, it stood upright and began to grow into a half-man, half-goat beast, complete with a human chest and hands, and cloven hooves with a furry waist. Its head also resembled that of a goat. Thick horns twisted from its skull.

It looked down on her.

"Ghurth tome da ratei, koliklee woa da norrgothen." it declared. Then, the beast produced a spiky wooden staff from thin air. Admiring its staff, the creature looked most pleased, as though it was just about to play after being in time-out for a very long time.

Its nostrils flared, then it raised the staff high over its head, preparing to swing down with the force of a god. Bethel closed her eyes and braced for impact.

CRACK!

The painful noise sounded like the clapping of thunder.

Yet Bethel felt no pain. She only felt something warm splatter on her face.

She slowly opened her eyes, only to see her sister's head had been bashed with the unholy stick. Indeed, Joanna's face was completely caved in. And more shocking, her body looked like it had prior to buying the book. Frail and malnourished.

The beast chortled with sinister pride, before raising its hands to exclaim: "Da porghatha jarr dee la!"

It turned and looked at Bethel, who was trembling in fear of her own life now. It looked down on her once again, like a master looks down on his dog.

"Pitiful woman," it uttered disparagingly in perfect English, "I can't stand the sight of someone as powerless as you."

"Don't kill me!" Bethel cried.

"Fool! I am not here to kill you. I am here to save you." the demonic goat threw its staff onto the floor. "Take this staff. With it, you can control your destiny."

Bethel scrambled on the floor like a desperate animal to collect her prize. She stroked the staff with intense pleasure.

"But know this—" the goat reminded. "—you received it... secondhand."

TYPHOON

It happened without warning. One fateful day, at three in the morning, a typhoon hit one of the largest metropolitan cities in the world. Usually residents would receive a notice of imminent weather disasters, especially something like a typhoon. Meteorologists the world over couldn't understand how the largest typhoon of the century could evade detection.

Try as they might, rescue workers were unable to enter the city for weeks, as the rain only let up during brief intervals of time in which any would-be rescuers entered only to find themselves swallowed up by gigantic whirlpools or other side effects of major flooding before the downpour of rainfall resumed again. An entire swath of civilization was wiped out.

Finally, after a month of being hammered by the storm, the city once again saw sunlight through the clouds. Well, the surface of the floodwater saw sunlight at least, as the city's skyline was submerged.

There were no survivors.

It took 40 days and nights before the floodwaters lowered, and another year before the water had completely evaporated. At that time, volunteers, researchers, and government officials were able to assess the damage.

They soon realized something astonishing. There were no bodies littering the streets, houses, or buildings. Nor were there any skeletal remains or anything suggesting any humans had died there.

After a while, the whole world began to forget about the disaster. It became something of an urban legend; many people questioned whether a typhoon had ever occurred. Eventually all of the city infrastructure disappeared and many people questioned whether a city had ever even existed there or not, too.

A new city was built in the same location a few decades later. Not overnight, of course, it started out small. Like any other town, it began with a few clusters of neighborhoods followed by general stores, hospitals, and such, until a whole new skyline was erected in place of the old, forgotten one.

Around that time, people began noticing strange phenomena taking place in the new city. White balls of light would lazily yet methodically float down the streets at night. A pattern started to arise where the ghostly orbs routinely traveled the same path every night. When sketched out, the path formed a circle around the entire city.

If that wasn't concerning enough, many residents also reported hearing the sound of wailing, usually around three in the morning, in both public and private places. What started out as a few isolated incidents soon became a relatively normal occurrence, as everyone living in the city started to hear the overpowering wailing clearly.

The only caveat was that people from out of town couldn't hear any such thing. To them, the locals were either stark-craving mad or simply trying to stir up excitement for tourism purposes. Like one big inside joke.

But it wasn't a joke at all. They really could hear something.

Over time, denizens of the city changed their names for no apparent reason. They just felt like it. Entire families changed their names, young and old alike.

They even started to change the way they looked, going so far as to receive plastic surgery until they were totally unrecognizable from their former selves.

Without even realizing it, the city became a carbon copy of the one preceding it. Every name. Every face. Exactly like the ones that had existed before. The ones that time had forgotten.

How long would it be until another event pushed the reset button? Until the city and those living within it would relive the same process over again?

More troublingly, how many other cities and people have experienced the same thing without ever knowing?

THAT WHICH REMAINS

I wake up in a dark room. My ears are ringing. My vision is full of static. As I try to make heads or tails of my surroundings, gradually, the static subsides and I ascend a staircase that reveals itself before me.

Reaching the top of the staircase, I find an empty classroom. I check the whiteboard where I see a disconcerting message written in blood: CHECK THE CLOSET.

I assume this is referring to the supply closet at the back of the room. With nothing else to do, I follow the directions on the board and proceed. I jiggle the stubborn handle until the closet door gives. It slowly opens.

A bloodied body falls out! It lies face down on the floor. Startled, I begin to flee on foot, until realizing something. That body looked awfully familiar. I stop in my tracks and turn around.

For several moments I do nothing but stare at the motionless body on the floor behind me. I walk back to determine if this body belongs to someone I know.

Upon turning it on its side, I immediately recognize its face.

It's an exact replica of myself. The spitting image of me. And it's lying dead before me. *How could this happen,* I think to myself. Suddenly, the corpse awakens! Its eyes glow yellow and it bares its teeth as it springs forward and lashes out at me. The sheer force of its attack pushes me to the floor.

Once again my eyesight starts to blur and becomes out of focus. The last thing I see clearly is the alternate version of myself – my evil twin – staring down, readying what looks like a blade to slash my throat or slice deep gashes across my face. Static takes over and I pass out as that familiar ringing noise returns to my eardrums. When my eyes re-open, I am not in the classroom. I'm safe in my bed. Relief washes over my body, but not for long. I cannot move. My entire body is paralyzed. I do my best to sit up, but it is impossible. I can't even wiggle my toes. My breathing grows heavy. I hope it doesn't stop.

Dark shadows dance around my bedside. Occasionally they whisper indecipherable nothings in my ear. Their aura feels hostile. I feel like they're teasing me the way some predators play with their prey before slaughtering it.

Something is rustling at the foot of the bed. I can't see it, but I can hear it. Now I can even feel it, touching my feet and moving up my legs and abdomen. It feels like it's crawling up the blanket covering my body, but I cannot move my neck to look down. Even if I could, I wouldn't dare.

I close my eyes as tight as I can. Whatever crawled up me is lying on top of me with its face hovering over my own. I can feel its breath. I can hear it grunting. I refuse to look out of fear of what I might see. Nothing good, I know.

Whatever it is, it starts to shake me violently from my shoulders down. Soon, I feel my whole body involuntarily flailing. The spasms are so intense that I am thrown onto the floor where my real torment begins.

Foolishly, I open my eyes. Or maybe they're forced open. I see myself lying on the floor, unresponsive. *Am I having an out-of-body experience?* A horrible epiphany dawns on me – I am *nothing*. A meaningless speck lying on a cold floor waiting to die if I haven't died already.

My family will never know what happened to me. They'll be distraught. Or perhaps they won't even notice my absence. Worse yet, perhaps they don't even exist. Maybe they never did. Maybe nothing does.

I feel total separation from God. Please, do not be so blind as to wince at my suggestion of God existing. Call it whatever you like. Call it the universe. Call it humanity. Call it life. Call it my ego. Whatever makes you *you*, makes reality *reality*, makes people *people*. Whatever *that* is, it's gone. And it may never come back, if it ever was here to begin with.

The shadows return for more cruel-spirited fun at my expense. They relish in my destruction and dance around the scraps of my smoldering existence. They pick away at what's left of my essence. All that remains is complete darkness and the inescapable feeling of being devoured from the inside out by these malevolent spirits.

Like worms, they bore through me.

So this is what dying feels like. It's worse than I could have ever imagined. Maybe if I stop struggling it'll be over soon. It'll all be over soon.

Finally, I return to my body. It jolts up, covered in cold sweat. I'm still on the floor, but I'm alive. I'm breathing. I calm down. Just as I suspected all long, this was only a sleep paralysis episode. They've been getting more horrific lately. I've endured them since I was in high school. Doctors told me they were nothing to worry about, that if I just slept on my side instead of on my back and if I eliminated stress from my life they would go away.

But they haven't gone away. They've only intensified. In the beginning, I just couldn't move for a few seconds. Seconds became minutes. Then I began having tactile hallucinations that gradually started to include auditory and visual components. Now, out-of-body experiences also often occur during my increasingly common sleep paralysis episodes.

Others who suffer from sleep paralysis tell me that it's all in our heads. That during this physical and mental state our bodies are just in transition between the conscious and subconscious world; they tell me that our brains temporarily paralyze our bodies during sleep so that we don't act out our dreams and inadvertently hurt ourselves or others — a preventative measure our bodies take to prevent sleepwalking and other sleep movement disorders. The hallucinations being mere manifestations of our subconscious played out in our half-awake environment. Since we are most likely to be scared when we find ourselves unable to move, our subconscious will generally, by default, conjure up scary images.

It all makes perfect sense on the surface. But I've done my best to stay positive and yet my hallucinations have only gotten worse. And why do they feel so real? I agree that the human brain is a powerful organ, capable of playing extremely convincing tricks on our perceptions of the world, but at what point am I allowed to feel that there might be something more external going on? That there really are dark forces afoot and that they want me dead...

I will go to the doctor again tomorrow.

MEME MAGICK

We're changing the world real quick
Using some of that old meme magick
Scroll on down, get lost in the spiral
It'll work once it's viral
Whether it's a sloth, cat, or frog
Each picture starts a new dialogue
Just imbue it with the occult
Then wrap it up in an insult
Change the way the masses think
Pull them back, away from the brink
It's been done for centuries
Reminds folks of their memories
Some may say that it sounds pagan
That we learned these tricks from evil Satan
I, for one, don't even disagree
But it feels so good to just be free
So let's make memes today, I say
Let's share them with our online prey
They don't know it now, but soon they'll see
We'll control their destiny
Each breath, each laugh, each wicked thought
We just love to stir the pot
Until reality is transformed
And to our bosom they have warmed
The ancient ones have foretold
Of what becomes of the uncontrolled
God forbid this knowledge is lost
For nowadays we live in chaos

Who among us can break the spell?
Can save us from our self-made hell?
The answer lies within the memes
Through them, you will achieve your dreams
Of course those dreams come at a toll
For one, you must become a troll

RISE OF THE TONGUE-EATERS

It all started early this spring. Claire had been swimming at the lake with her friends. Nothing out of the ordinary happened, other than maybe a few French kisses she snuck in with her sweetheart, Rodney. The two of them had found a secret cubbyhole behind a large rock formation that their friends were using as a starting point to launch themselves into the murky water.

Beyond making out, Claire simply enjoyed spending time with her friends. They playfully splashed each other and enjoyed some homemade sandwiches on the lakeshore.

On their way home, Claire sat in the backseat of her friend's Pontiac. She noticed a slight tingling pain in the sides of her lower jaw, but brushed it off as a mere side effect of her migraines.

However, as the week progressed, the pain only worsened. It was painful to move her jaw at all, let alone to open her mouth. The pain had spread up to her ear canal.

Her family physician examined the insides of her ears. He noted there was some inflammation and explained that she was suffering from a condition known as "swimmer's ear" - an unpleasant affliction in which small amounts of water become lodged within one's ears and sometimes cause infection.

The doctor gave her some ear drop medication and told her that it would help dry out the trapped water. He assured her this would also clear up any irritation in her jaw line.

She was satisfied with his explanation and eager to go home and test out the ear drops. He recommended she only put a single drop into each ear every few hours, but after noticing little to no effect, she began applying more drops in a desperate attempt to clear out the infection.

But it was to no avail.

The pain only worsened over time and spread from her ears and jaw to her tongue. She sobbed and complained to her family. Sometimes it was too excruciatingly painful to complain, so she could only let out high-pitched wheezes. She was in no state to go to school. All she could do was stay at home and wait out her affliction alone.

Five weeks after going to the lake, the pain had nearly reached its limit when it suddenly stopped. Overnight, the pain vanished. It was replaced by numbness. Whereas before she could feel every sting and tingle in her oral nerves, now she felt nothing. It was paradoxically both a relief and a source of even more concern for Claire.

Everything came to a disturbing climax when, over dinner, she tried to tell her family that she had lost all sensation in her mouth, jaws, tongue, and throat. But unable to feel her tongue, her words came out slurred.

Suddenly, she started coughing up blood onto her plate. Her mother raced to her side with a roll of paper towels to clean up the mess as blood poured out of her mouth like a red waterfall. So much blood was pouring out that her father decided paper towels weren't enough.

He fetched a bucket and placed it under her chin.

More blood spilled into the bucket, nearly filling it up half-way. By now, Claire was beginning to look pale. Her skin was losing color with each drop of blood.

Finally, the blood flowing from her mouth slowed from a steady surge to a slow trickle until it stopped entirely.

Splunk!

Something solid fell into the bucket.

Claire's parents dared to look inside and fish out the object.

It was her tongue.

Totally severed from her oral cavity.

Her tongue.

As if it had been cut from her mouth with a crude device like a pair of rusty scissors.

All Claire could do now was moan a ghastly moan. She was too lightheaded to comprehend what was happening, but her parents witnessed it all with vivid clarity.

Claire leaned back and opened her mouth. Then, her mother and father saw it. Her new tongue.

It looked like a parasitic bug. Almost like a fully white cicada. And it had replaced her tongue with itself, using her head as its shell. It lunged out at the table and snatched the food that was left on her plate before retracting back into her mouth.

Her parents rushed her to the emergency room. An MRI revealed that Claire's mouth, and indeed her entire skull, was being hollowed out to host this parasite.

Doctors tried to remove it with prongs and other tools at their disposal, but there was a legitimate concern that the parasite was the only thing keeping her alive at the moment and that if this symbiotic relationship was interrupted it would result in her death.

She was kept overnight for observation.

The next morning, a nurse noticed Claire's head was missing. It had been totally dislodged from her neck. Spinal fluid was leaking onto the floor from the pillow where her head once lay.

Security guards checked the CCTV footage and concluded that her head had turned at an 180 degree angle and crawled out of the bed and into an air vent on its own, but the doctors knew better. It hadn't turned on its own. She had been decapitated by the parasite, which crawled away using her head as its new home like a hermit crab uses bottle caps or anything else it can find.

A maintenance man was called in to investigate the ventilation ducts. He wasn't told that he was looking for the disembodied head of a young woman, just that there might be a rodent or some other pest inside and he needed to capture it.

Hours passed without his return. Either something horrible had happened to him, or he was lost in the ventilation system. Then, the overpowering stench of death filled each room of the hospital, seemingly distributed through the air ducts.

Dark blood started dripping from one of the outlet diffusers in the hospital cafeteria. Members of the staff placed a ladder underneath and climbed up to open the large duct. Inside was the maintenance man. Dead.

His entire lower jaw and tongue were missing, completely ripped from his face.

As the hospital director attempted to keep everyone calm and maintain order in the building, a pathologist examined Claire's headless body. He wanted to be the first to discover any new organisms that might be dwelling within her.

Through her neck-hole, he noticed several abnormal growths, but nothing could prepare him for what he was about to find inside. Immediately upon cutting through her torso, a large black hive of flying parasites exploded from her body and engulfed the pathologist.

As he screamed, they entered through his mouth and any other orifice that was available. He was to be their new live host.

Unbeknownst to the outside world, this was ground zero for a new species of parasites.

The tongue-eaters.

———————

THE SOUP LADY OF DIYU

There are many courts in Diyu, the realm of the dead. One day you will know this for yourself to be true. Until then, you will have to rely on the ancestral knowledge that has been passed down from generation to generation. Of the many courts in Diyu, one of the last you will enter before arriving in the realm of the living is the eighteenth court.

There you will meet Meng Po. The Lady of Forgetfulness. Or, as some affectionately call her, the Soup Lady. That last moniker is the most fitting, the reason being is that she serves a most potent soup to every soul before it is reborn. It's her specialty: the Five Flavored Soup of Forgetfulness. This soup is so powerful, it causes anyone who ingests it to completely forget all remnants of his or her past life. With a clean slate, they can receive a new earthly incarnation and begin life anew.

Of course, concocting this magical brew is no easy task. Meng Po must first fetch all of the required ingredients from rare mineral water based in a limited number of streams. Gathering ingredients is just one step in the process. Combining them takes special precision that even the most advanced of technologies cannot achieve.

Once the soup is prepared, it must be served at just the right temperature, and it is only effective for one week. After that, a new batch must be made. Her cafeteria in that little corner of the eighteenth court of hell serves millions of souls each year.

Needless to say, it's a difficult and thankless job. One that, after thousands of years of service, Meng Po finally grew tired of one day.

It wasn't just the job, though. It was a culmination of factors. A big one being that she had met a man while cultivating ingredients for the soup. A man whom she had fallen deeply in love with. She hoped to be betrothed to him soon. Surely, she thought, she could resign from her position and enjoy at least one normal life.

She brought this matter to the attention of Zhuang Lun Wang. Zhuang Lun was her superior; more than that, he was a god. The god presiding over her department. Being the god responsible for the eighteenth court of the realm of the dead, Zhuang Lun was and is the decider of fates.

He has access to everyone's record. Each life. Each action. Each indiscretion. Everything. Taking all of this into account, he decides where each soul will be reborn. To many he is regarded as tough but fair. Meng Po had worked alongside him long enough to, she thought, get on his good side.

She seemed to be highly favored among her peers.

Zhuang Lun considered her situation carefully. He assessed her record, one of the cleanest to ever grace the surface of his desk. Her years of faithful service. Her impeccable talent. Her professionalism. She was definitely indispensable, but she had also definitely earned a break.

After reflecting on her request, he made a decision.

He would allow her to resign and marry her lover, but on one condition: like every other soul, she had to drink the soup first.

Meng Po thought long and hard about this stipulation. She worried that, without her memory, she would forget her future husband. But this fear quickly melted away as she considered the facts. In her mind, her star-crossed lover and her were destined to be together.

If none other than Zhuang Lun Wang was granting her this opportunity, he must have known as well as she did that her love was pure, why else would he allow her this chance? With not only her own intuition, but the blessing of a god, she was willing to forfeit all of her memories. Fate had led her here and fate would lead her back to her soulmate.

After this quick deliberation, she agreed to Zhuang Lun's precondition and took a sip of her own special soup. A sip was all that was needed to purge her memories. She felt fresh.

She looked up at Zhuang Lun and asked what her purpose was. Normally this was when he would spin the wheel of life to help determine her position, but for Meng Po he would make an exception.

"What is my fate?" she asked again.

Zhuang Lun Wang pointed to the kitchen. "You're the soup lady. Get back to work."

UNTITLED 1

In the aftermath of a gruesome murder, most investigators start their journey into the macabre world of the killer by securing the crime scene. Ty Anderson was no exception. His job was not one for the faint of heart, and he was reminded of that fact on Thursday, August 19th as he unrolled barricade tape with the phrase *CRIME SCENE DO NOT CROSS* printed in all caps along the outside parameter of a house on Cedar Street. And what a crime scene it was. The air even smelled of it with a distinct, musky mixture of moldy dust and the putrid scent of a rotting body lingering in the residence. It was that smell which seeped through the thick walls and was noticed by neighbors who had called in the suspicious odor to authorities. Beyond that hideous smell which Ty had become accustomed to, the victim's face was the next thing he noticed. It was peeled clean off with almost surgical precision. This wasn't the perpetrator's first rodeo, they most certainly had done it before.

The victim's face wasn't the only thing missing. His manhood was also unaccounted for. Probably nailed to a two-by-four in some dusty cellar or frying in a pan over a greasy stove by now. An incision had been made right above the crotch in the lower belly area. Ty would get to that later, but for the next few minutes he started to evaluate the possibilities. It didn't appear as though there had been a struggle – nothing in the room was out of place or disheveled. Other than the aforementioned mutilations, there were no scratch marks or defense wounds present on the body. No traces of blood in other parts of the vicinity that would indicate the victim had tried to flee. No shell casings.

The killer was nothing short of a professional, but then again, so was Ty. He took out his Canon EOS and started taking pictures. He loved taking pictures. When he was in the sixth grade he wanted to be a photographer. He had used up countless rolls of 35 millimeter film from disposable cameras. His mother was none too pleased. It was her opinion that he should be aiming for loftier ambitions like becoming an architect or a proctologist. She often scowled upon seeing photographs of leaves and ponds plastered in his room. A photographer was no kind of job to make a living. Luckily for her, he didn't become a photographer. Still, those skills he honed in his youth didn't go to waste. There he was snapping away at the shutter release. His model being the poor dead schmuck on the floor.

As the camera flash briefly illuminated the room with an explosion of light, he saw something shiny reflect like a pocket mirror from the incision on the victim's lower abdomen. He examined the incision more closely. There was something sticking out from the inside. It was an SD card. Its copper pins were the source of the reflection earlier. In all his years of service, Ty had never tampered with evidence, but something about this small digital chip beckoned him. He was a professional, he shouldn't have been open to temptation… but he nonetheless was. After taking a big gulp of saliva that tasted of the dust and death he was breathing in, he produced a pair of tweezers from his array of tools and carefully picked out the SD card like a vulture picking out a particularly succulent strip of meat from a carcass's bones. He delicately placed the card inside a tiny Ziploc bag. Something about this felt wrong. Of course it did, it *was* wrong. Ty was going to keep this piece of evidence for himself and he knew it, but he didn't know why. He did know he needed a cigarette, though.

Placing the evidence in his pocket, he walked outside for a smoke. With the cig loosely gripped between his lips, he lifted the lighter to its tip and cuffed it under the protection of his hand to fend off any stray breeze that might extinguish the flame. Just as he was about to light the sucker, he glanced at the crawlspace underneath the porch of the residence. Had he been a superstitious man he would have felt that something was pulling him towards it; since he wasn't, however, he just felt that he gravitated towards it on his own accord. A breeze that would have put out his cigarette had he lit it instead lightly pushed him closer. He removed some cinder blocks that were blocking entry to the crawlspace under the house and peered inside. It was pitch dark. Although the weather that night wasn't particularly cold, he could see his breath in the air. Each puff of breath drifted into the dark crawlspace and became absorbed by the darkness. He pulled out his tactical flashlight to assess the environment. Its beams uncovered everything that was hiding in the shadowy space beneath the house.

A bunch of concrete slabs. Scraps of pink fiberglass

clinging to the foundation. Old kickballs and a naked doll missing its head.

And a body. A human body that was lying on its side. A body that Ty could only see from behind. It looked as though it was curled up in the fetal position. Chunks of skin were missing from its back and arched shoulders. Maggots were feasting on its decaying husk. The skin looked like it would easily peel off its rotting flesh and bones.

The light flickered and went out. His peepshow was over whether he liked it or not, but with a few smacks the flashlight beamed again. He directed the light back at the body. Its position had changed. Not only had it inched closer to him, but it had also shifted so that it was facing him directly. Except it didn't have a face.

Ty shot backwards, falling on his ass and shuffling away from the dank crawlspace. Hell, away from the damned house in general.

In all of his years as a crime scene investigator, this was the most bizarre experience he had ever endured. It was a night of many firsts. The first time he found someone without a face. *Two* someones without a face. The first time he concealed evidence for personal use. The first time that… whatever had just happened had happened.

He decided to check on the body in the crawlspace one more time. Of course, he was careful not to get too close this time. Shining the flashlight from a safe distance, he looked back inside. The body was gone. Disappeared without a trace. His eyes must have played a trick on him before. Happens all the time out in the field. Well, it had never happened to him before (as previously mentioned this was a night of firsts), but he had heard colleagues speaking about similar tricks their eyes had played on them in the field.

He went back into the house, totally forgetting his cigarette. Nicotine could wait, but his job couldn't. It was time to wrap this up so the coroner's office could take in another body for examination. But it wasn't meant to be. Upon returning to the room where the original body was, the body that he had been called to investigate the death of, he found that it, too, had vanished. Another first.

Ty switched on his camera's menu to look through the photos, but they had all been replaced by images of himself holding a flashlight and looking into the crawlspace. His hair stood on the nape of his neck as he scrolled through the photographs, trying to conjure up an explanation. There was even a decent shot of him looking terrified before falling backwards.

He rang his supervisor.

"Hey Tom, about that crime scene on Cedar Street," he said uneasily, "It's getting intense. I might need some assistance."

"Very funny, Ty. I'd be laughing if I didn't have papers on my desk right now, important shit to do. There haven't been any calls on Cedar Street tonight. That's one of the safest streets in Ottawa. Besides, dispatch would've sent you, not me."

Ty checked his call log. "I see it here. In my phone's history. A call from you at eight-thirty tonight. I'll send you the screenshot to prove it." He followed through and snapped a screenshot, which he immediately forwarded to Tom via text. He could hear Tom's phone vibrating on the other line, along with Tom's exasperated sigh.

"Ty... there's no call from me in this screenshot." Tom shot back his own screencap of Ty's original, but this time it was missing Tom's call in the log. "And aren't you supposed to be on vacation?"

Ty searched through his memory. He *was* supposed to be on vacation.

"Look, I appreciate your sense of humor, but I have to get back to work. Don't waste my time with any more of this nonsense." With those parting words, Tom abruptly hung up.

It took a few minutes for Ty to compose himself enough to stumble outside again. He shuffled to his Dodge and crawled in, defeated.

Nonsense.

How embarrassing.

This was the first time Tom had hung up on him like that. And the first time he had given Tom a reason to. He should've known something was amiss when he arrived and nobody else was there. No police officers or first responders.

Ty put the van into gear and drove home.

Country songs played on the radio as he tightly gripped the steering wheel. If he couldn't calm his nerves, maybe Reba McEntire could as she serenaded him about a fateful night in Georgia. Somehow it seemed appropriate, this was proving to be a fateful night for him as well. Within fifteen minutes he was in the den of his home. Although the evening had been a terrifying crapshoot so far, he tried to look back and piece it all together. He had to prove to himself that he wasn't crazy.

Then he remembered... the SD card. He reached into his pocket and felt the Ziploc bag. He pulled it out and lifted it up to eye level. The SD card was inside. At least there was something that was real from tonight. He moseyed over to his desktop computer and shoved the card into the tower. Soon, its contents brightly displayed on the screen before him.

Three folders:

a *OPEN TONIGHT*
b *OPEN TOMORROW*
c *DON'T OPEN*

Curious, he clicked on the first folder. OPEN TONIGHT. He always was good at following orders. Inside the folder were several pictures. Normal pictures. Pictures of a man on vacation in Italy. He was posing by iconic spots like Amalfi Coast and the Florence Cathedral. He seemed happy enough. Ty continued scrolling through the pictures until he realized the man in them looked familiar. He squinted to make out more details of the fellow's face. If he didn't know any better, it looked like one of his old high school classmates. Rodger Sailler. Or as he used to call him, 'Rodge'. Rodge must have been doing okay for himself, Mr. World Traveler.

There weren't that many pictures, but he was smiling in all of them. Except one. The last one in the folder. It was a picture of Rodge — bloody, dead, and lying on the grass in a field somewhere. Carved into his chest was the following symbol:

Ty stared at it. Mesmerized. The alchemical symbol for sulfur. How did he instinctively know that? How did his brain recognize it without question? He sat back in his chair and rubbed his chin. So much for a reunion… Rodge from high school was dead as a door nail. Yet, despite not seeing Rodge for well over a decade, snapshots of his life and final moment were in Ty's home on an SD card that he had found on a dead body at a crime scene that didn't exist.

He leaned back in his chair and took a deep breath. Tempted as he was, he didn't open the second folder. Instead, he turned off the computer monitor and went to take an overdue shower where he could forget all of his troubles for a few fleeting moments.

After the shower, he felt ethereal, as though he was untouchable. Any remnants of concern pertaining to recent events in his life had melted away, leaving a soft, blubbery core in their place. Ty Anderson was at peace. He quickly fell asleep, quicker than usual, and drifted into another space of consciousness. One where his old classmate Rodger Sailler was still alive. He couldn't see that it was Rodge, but he knew it was Rodge.

Instinctively.

"You left us, Ty."

"Left who? We were just classmates, man."

"*Just?* Shit, you're even loonier than I thought. That headmaster must have done a number on you."

"What headmaster?"

"You don't remember Travis Draper? He was our headmaster. The whole reason you got into forensic science. For the Dark One, brother. We all must play our part. I played mine faithfully, now it is your turn."

"Mr. Draper?" Ty flew through his old memory reservoir — searching. "He was our homeroom teacher. I haven't heard from him in ages."

"You always were his favorite. Maybe that's why you don't remember. Maybe he decided to spare you the painful memories. The nightmares. The knowledge of what's to come. But come hell or high water, it *will* come, Ty. No one is safe. Not even you. Just accept it when it happens, you'll be better off for it. Like me."

"I think I'm starting to remember, Rodge. We were part of an after-school club. Travis Draper was in charge..."

"Stop. Don't go any further. Ignorance is bliss, Ty."

Ty didn't wake up. He simply opened his eyes — softly yet abruptly, he opened his eyes. The lights were all off, save for the glow from his computer screen in the den. Silly him, he had forgotten to turn it off. He pulled himself out of bed. He remembered falling asleep, but he didn't recall falling asleep in bed. Never mind that, he had to turn off that damned computer. At moments like this, he wished he had a wife and kids. Maybe if he did, he could yell at one of his kids to turn it off for him. But he had neither wife nor offspring. Or did he? Why did he feel like he did? Never mind. That frikkin' light from the computer was enough to drive him mad. He walked down the hallway and to the living room, making a bee-line for the box of circuits.

Before he turned it off, however, he looked at the screen. The SD folder's window was still open and the second folder caught his eye.

OPEN TOMORROW.

Say, what was the date? He checked the bottom of the screen. By now, today would be tomorrow. Early tomorrow, for sure, but tomorrow nonetheless. Ty was always good at following directions. He sat down in the folded chair in front of his computer (because he was too cheap to buy a swivel chair) and opened the folder. Just as expected, there were pictures inside, but their thumbnails didn't show any images so he clicked on the first one to take a gander. Oh, it wasn't a picture after all, it was a video. And his computer didn't have the right software to view it. He was sure he had installed the media player when he bought the computer... either way, it wasn't a big deal. A few clicks later and he was able to watch the first video.

It was a video of Rodge surrounded by men wearing long, hooded robes. Rodge knelt in the center of the video as the robed men formed a circle around him. He seemed out of it, like in a trance, swaying side to side as if in a drunken stupor, while guttural chants bellowed from the men. A ring of fire slowly began to rise from the ground, seemingly on its own as nobody in the camera's view had started it. The flames rose higher and higher until Rodge could no longer be seen. Finally, the chants stopped, and with them, the fire. Immediately after the chorus ended and the flames died, Rodge was revealed once more. Except this time he was not in a trance, nor was his body swaying. Instead, it was motionless and stiff. And on his chest was the same symbol Ty had seen on his corpse in the picture from before. The video cut to black.

Ty sat in his chair, scared and confused. The picture was unsettling, but the video was downright chilling. And there were still three more videos to go.

He contemplated his life for a moment. Specifically this moment of it. Then, he clicked on the next video.

This one was also of Rodge, who was now lying on his back in the grass, bleeding from the symbol that had somehow been cut into his body's frontal frame. The symbol wasn't the only area that was bleeding. So was Rodge's forehead. And then his temples. And chin. A thin line of red circled around his face, as if someone was using a red pen to trace a line there. Slowly, his face – the skin of it at least – began to rise from his skull. It hovered above its old home and lifted into the air by itself. It looked like a mask. Like the work of a phantom Hannibal Lecter. Ty's brow furrowed as he tried to analyze the video. He couldn't believe that someone's face could just peel off on its own like that. This had to be the work of special effects. Someone was playing a very elaborate prank on him. There was no way this could be real, right?

There were only two possible explanations: either it was real, or it wasn't. If it wasn't, it must have taken a lot of time and money to put together. If it was...

... then it had to be supernatural. And that didn't sit well with Ty. Being a man of science who had spent countless times in the vicinity of dead bodies and had never had anything close to a spiritual experience, he couldn't wrap his mind around this being real. Still, instead of questioning it further, he clicked on the second video in the folder.

This one was of an older gentleman wearing a suit, tie, and bowler hat. A bit gaudy, but the old timer pulled it off. He was sitting down and looking directly into the camera. No flashy background, just a white wall.

"I'm only going to say this once, so listen up and listen well. And please remember this. Take it to heart." the old man said solemnly, "I'm sorry, Ty."

Ty shot back in his chair. Luckily it was there or he'd have fallen on his ass again. How did this old guy know his name? He replayed the video.

"I'm only going to say this once, so listen up and listen well. And please remember this. Take it to heart. I'm sorry, Ty."

He moved the scrollbar back a tad, he only wanted to catch the tail-end of the video.

"I'm sorry, Ty."

Well, he definitely said Ty's name, that was unquestionable. More than anything else, this was when things started to feel real and tangible. Ty had no idea who that man was, but whoever he was he certainly knew Ty somehow. That was scarier than seeing Rodge die in a ritual sacrifice. Scarier than any of the cases he had investigated over the years.

With some trepidation, he clicked on the last video.

It was from the crawlspace. The one he had shone a flashlight in on Cedar Street. This was the same video he had on his camera before, of himself falling backwards. But this time, the video continued playing longer. It showed the empty front yard of the residence, and eventually, showed Ty walking back to his truck and driving away.

Then it ended.

And Ty felt something deep in his gut. Something he thought he had conquered a long time ago, but apparently hadn't. He felt fear. Real fear. Primal fear. Not just because he was being hunted, evidently, but because that old man wearing the bowler hat had apologized directly to him. Apologized for what? The contrast of that old fellow against the horror of the other videos put him off more than anything.

Then he looked at the screen once more and saw that final unopened folder.

DON'T OPEN.

He knew he shouldn't. He knew opening that would lead to his certain death. There was no need to explain, he just knew it the way a newborn baby knows to cry for attention or a duckling knows to follow its mother. It was just a fact. If he clicked on that folder, he would die a horrible death. Not just horrible, but grisly and terrifying. One that might haunt him for many lives to come and would certainly make this life end on a sour note. Besides, he was good at following directions. The folder said DON'T OPEN, so he wouldn't open it.

Instead, he opened a blank document and began typing. It didn't take him long, no more than ten minutes. When he was finished, he clicked 'close', and when prompted, he saved the document. Outside of photography, he never was much of a creative type, so he didn't go through the trouble of giving the document a proper title. Even if he had been a creative type, he wouldn't have given it a title. He didn't have time.

He was ending this. He was ending it now. And he was ending it on his terms.

After saving the untitled document, he sat up from his chair and walked into the kitchen. The last sounds he heard were his own footsteps on the tiled floor, the opening of the kitchen pantry where he kept his revolver, and the final cocking of said revolver before raising it to his temple and blowing his own brains out.

Whoever or whatever wanted him wouldn't get him this time. Or so he thought. Perhaps they were waiting for him on the other side. Still, at least he got to feel like he was in control of those final moments.

When investigators walked onto the scene of Ty Anderson's suicide, it looked like an open-and-shut case. The SD card in his computer was empty of the contents that had pushed him to take his own life. The only thing they found to shed light on his state of mind was a file called 'Untitled 1'.

It was a suicide note, and a pretty standard one at that. His immediate supervisor confirmed Ty had been acting differently and nobody ever questioned the events surrounding his untimely demise.

———◦———

TALE OF THE PORONEIC

Many moons ago, in what is the present-day territory of Slovakia, a gruff-looking man was collecting kindling to warm his family's cabin. It was a small cabin, one he had built with his own two hands. The cabin was as simple as the times they were living in. Earlier in the day he had been tending to a tiny plot of land, planting seeds for harvest later in the year, so his dirty, gray work shirt tightly clung to his sweaty back. Tied around his waist were a few dead rabbits he had killed. They, along with some cabbage, would be dinner tonight.

His faithful and hardworking housewife was waiting for him back at home. Just as he had tended to the land, she had tended to their newborn son. Nursing him, singing Slavic lullabies to him, holding down the fort until the love of her life returned. Well, in those days marriage was less out of love and more out of necessity. The necessity to survive. One couldn't very well survive without some sort of binding agreement to keep two people saddled together through the good and bad. In those days, they understood that talk comes cheap. That everything in life boils down to a business negotiation. A way of holding everyone accountable to their words.

Still, the two of them shared a stronger bond that more closely resembled our modern idea of love than most other married couples of their time. Maybe because they had experienced the trauma of losing their firstborn who was born dead. Hours after going into labor, and after painful contractions, the stillborn baby emerged with its own umbilical cord wrapped around its tiny neck – strangled.

For the first time in her hard-boiled life, the mother wept uncontrollably. It took six nights for her to accept what had happened. During those six miserable nights, they didn't bury the body. They kept it close, beside their bed. Sometimes the mother would fall sleep with it in her arms. It wasn't until she started having nightmarish visions of the baby killing her in her sleep that she agreed to give it a burial. Both young, her and her husband buried it outside near a pond that wasn't far from their cabin. As a marker, they placed a few sticks and stones on the mound of dirt that was its burial site.

Through it all, the man cherished his grieving wife. She took the brunt of the emotional trauma inflicted by their loss, which he admired her for. He admired her capacity to care so deeply. In many ways, that experience was what made their bond stronger than most. They didn't have time to dwell on it, however, as it wasn't long after that ordeal that she was pregnant again. Nine months later, that baby was born healthy. That baby was safe and sound at home.

As that baby's father looked out at what would later be known as the Tatra Mountains, he felt it was time to go home too. He had gathered enough wood for a fire. Not only that, but he had some intuition that he was needed. People were more attached to nature in those days, to Earth itself, so back then our intuitions were sharper. More organic. Less polluted by all the distractions of today. His family needed him now. He prayed to Perun that they were okay.

Meanwhile, back home, his wife prayed to Perun for his return. The baby hadn't cried all day. He hadn't even nursed. Her breasts felt neglected. Worse, *she* felt neglected. By her own infant son, no less. This was very abnormal behavior for him, and she suspected, for any baby. The little one had instead been staring at the door all day, almost without blinking. At times she worried he had slipped away into the afterlife, but upon closer examination he was always breathing. Silently waiting and watching for something. She wiped the slobber from his chin, but he did not react at all. He didn't even notice. She moved him to the bed, but he would crawl down and return to his old position a few feet away from the door and resume gazing at it.

Outside, the father was approaching home. He was circling around the pond now, but before he could continue, something caught his attention. The marker for his dead child's grave was gone. The same marker he had seen every day for the past year. The same one that had always reminded him of his marriage's defining moment. It was gone. Not just the marker, but the mound it perched on, too. The entire grave, small as it was, was gone. It had been dug up, leaving an empty hole in the dirt. *The foxes must have dug it up for food*, he thought. Still, deep down he knew it wasn't so simple. If foxes or other animals had wanted to dig up his dead child, they would've already done it long ago. He picked up his pace.

The door was open when he arrived at the cabin, a trail of blood led inside. He quickly dropped his kindling and ran in. The scene was gory. Entrails laced the floor, chairs, and table that that he had built. Pieces of his lovely wife were strewn about the interior of their home. He briefly bowed his head, almost as though he was in prayer. A fleeting moment of solitude in remembrance of his beloved. It was soon interrupted by a gurgling sound in the sleeping area. Tiny, bloody footprints led to that area as well.

He grabbed a fire iron that had been lying on the floor, seemingly used by his dearly departed wife, and clinched it tightly with his sweaty hands as he cautiously stepped towards what could be called the bedroom, following the footprints. The source of the disturbing sound was nowhere to be seen. The footprints ended abruptly at the foot of the handcrafted bed. The sound stopped too. He could only hear his own heart beating wildly like a drum.

It seemed as though he was alone. In the back of his mind he wondered where his son was and if he was all right. Then, he registered something jerking at his waist, a light tug. Something was pulling at one of the dead rabbits strapped to him. He jumped back and readied the fire iron. What he saw sent a chill up his old-world spine. It was a demonic-looking troglodyte, purple in color with a disgusting slit in the middle of its deformed mouth full of jagged canines and stubby molars that were sticking out like sore thumbs. A leathery tongue drooped from its God-forsaken face. Its eyes were entirely black. Drool spilled from its mouth and onto the hardwood floor. That gurgling sound came back, obviously from this wretched demon. He realized then that the gurgling noise was the sound of its labored breathing combined with it choking on its own saliva. Its lower jaw was barely visible, if at all.

He swung at it, but then jumped back before making contact. He may have been the kind of man they don't make any more, but he wasn't going to chance death. God only knew what would happen if he made any kind of contact with that thing. Seething with unadulterated anger, it growled an angry growl. He dared not take his eyes off of it. He knew that the longer he stared at it, the higher the likelihood would be that its image would be burned into his memory and haunt his dreams, but he was more worried about it lunging for his jugular if he let his guard down.

He noticed something was hanging from its neck. Something that resembled a rope that had rotted down to its last remaining fibers.

It was then that he knew this was no ordinary demon. It was his own flesh and blood, come back from the grave, complete with its umbilical cord still wrapped around its decomposing neck. It was a poroneic. A malicious demon formed from the remains of dead children, especially dead babies. *Especially* dead babies that had been improperly buried. Unlike most other people in his time, he had always considered them nothing but an old wives' tale. Love wasn't the only thing that set him apart from others, lack of superstitious belief also did, until that moment. And from what he remembered, a poroneic was exponentially more powerful than the average demon due to its sheer potential. Within each poroneic was all the unused energy of an entire life just waiting to be tapped into.

The poroneic bolted towards its father, the very man whom it owed its existence to, and screeched as it lunged towards his face – claws extending from its baby-like fingers. In vain, he whacked it with the fire iron. It didn't even leave a dent. The poroneic was on top of him as he lay on the floor in the most vulnerable position one could be in any fight, let alone a fight with this creature.

The tyrant could have killed him then and there with a simple thrashing from its ever-protruding claws or a quick bite from its bacteria-infested teeth. Instead, it chose to prolong his suffering and reached for the fire iron. It intended to do him in as he had previously planned to do it in.

Gripping the sharp metal rod in its chubby, fleshy mitts, it raised it up like a spear — readying to thrust it into his petrified face. Its diabolic gurgles began to sound like mutated chuckles.

Just as it was about to pulverize him, a woman entered the fray. It was none other than his wife. Both he and the poroneic froze and looked at her with reverence. The awe-inspired expression on each of their faces looked as though they were watching a heavenly angel walk into the room. It was then that the man realized his wife had not been killed after all. It had been their son who was the real victim of the vengeful sibling. Their only healthy son whose guts had been ripped out and sprawled across the cabin.

He half-expected his wife to come charging at the barbaric beast-child. Perhaps they could overpower it and vanquish it forever. Perhaps they could start anew after this.

She didn't charge at it though, nor did she even let on any sign of anger or spitefulness.

She merely opened her arms in the most motherly fashion. The poroneic dropped the fire iron, which narrowly missed the man's head and fell on the floor, and slowly stood up. Step by step, it walked to its mother with outreached arms. She embraced it with love and understanding, and, lifting it up, bared her right breast so that it could feed. And feed it did. Ugly as it was, it quietly fed on her breast milk like a healthy baby would do – suckling on the bounty of her bosom.

The man felt as though he had lost his mind. Was this to be their future? To care for this abomination? Could he accept his resurrected prodigal child that had killed its own kin? He stood up as he contemplated these questions and steadily approached his wife who seemed to have no qualms with accepting this… thing that she had wept for a year prior. This demon whose corpse she had slept beside for six nights.

The poroneic sensed his approach and recoiled, hissing at him as he inched closer. Its dark, soulless eyes would have pierced through him if he had anything left in his heart or mind for them to pierce through. The mother softly shushed it.

The man lowered his head at the level of her exposed breasts. One of them was still vacant and stiff, waiting to be sucked dry. Like an infant, the burly man stood across from his demon spawn and suckled on his deranged wife's breast as she cackled victoriously in a perverted scene that would send them all to hell eventually.

Outside, by the pond, several boginki (demonic deities that often lived near water in those days) celebrated by singing to the full moon, which was casting an abnormally bright light onto the simple cabin that night.

THE MANDELA EFFECT

Davina Lynn will never forget the day she heard the news. She was sitting in a wooden swing on her porch, racking her brain over how she would pay the electric bill for the month. Not just the current month, but the past three months. Every day felt like a roll of the proverbial dice, a pull of the slot machine lever as to whether it would be the day the power would be cut off. God knew she needed that power for at least another two weeks so she could continue hunting for a job (she had been unemployed for over a year). Her online applications hadn't borne any fruit yet, but access to the web was the only string keeping her tethered to any hope for a chance at landing a job. She couldn't use a public library computer as there wasn't one of those for miles, and even if there was it wouldn't have made much of a difference as she was without a car, friends, or any other means of transportation.

Perhaps that was why the news felt like such an insurmountable burden to bear. It was 12:40 P.M. on a Wednesday when she received a call on her pre-paid phone. Not just a call, *the* call. The call that changed her life. She lifted the handheld rectangle to her ear and uttered a barely audible greeting.

The voice on the other end sounded both consolatory but business-like. It was a woman's voice. "Ms. Lynn, this is Dr. Joyce Carter. Your father checked into Montgomery Memorial Hospital last Friday complaining of chest pain. He listed you as the only emergency contact on his patient check-in form." Davina could hear the intimidating echo of the hospital intercom paging for a nurse in the background, along with a myriad of other noises – from the sound of carts of medicine trays being shuffled around, to a variety of beeping sounds. She regained focus on the voice as it continued. "He's in a lot of distress. Could you please come to the hospital?"

Davina's mind had wandered halfway around the world and back again in the fraction of a second. The phone slid down her right cheek and fell into her lap. Later on, when asked about this incident, she didn't remember hanging up, she just remembered walking. Walking to Montgomery Memorial Hospital. It took her forty minutes to arrive in the lobby where she was greeted by hospital staff and taken up to a room on the fourth floor where her father was lying in a small bed. Dozens of thin plastic tubes were intravenously pumping his lifeless body full of God only knows what. For his sake, hopefully morphine. Davina cuffed her hands over her mouth and gasped as tears began to blur her vision of her deceased father lying before her.

The doctor informed her that he had died from complications of a myocardial infarction, commonly known as a heart attack. She was his next of kin, but she didn't have any money to hold a funeral service. She thought maybe she could use whatever was left in his estate to cover the cost of burying him, but it seemed poverty ran in the family. He didn't have so much as a red cent left to his name when he kicked the bucket.

Considering her own financial strains, she almost wished it had been her dead body lying in the bed. She had been robbed of even the most basic components of human dignity: the ability to mourn the passing of a loved one. There would be no time for mourning the loss of her father – only time for crowdfunding through any means necessary in order to lay him to rest. Her job hunt would have to wait. The hospital agreed to store her father's body in the morgue until she could find the means to respectfully dispose of the body.

Too tired to cry, she walked home with a dark cloud hanging over her head. Not literally, of course, but figuratively. She reckoned the best way to raise funds would be to ask for money online. It wasn't ideal, but it was her only choice on such short notice. She would fire up the old Windows 7 and go online as soon as she got home.

At the time she finally did arrive at her house, she found a flaw in her plan when she went to turn on the light switch to her living room. *Click!* Nothing but a dark void. *Click! Click! Click!* She frantically flipped the switch over and over, but to no avail. The power had been cut off. No power meant no access to her computer, which meant her new task of burying her dead father just became ten times more strenuous. Davina violently hurled her keys into the dark void of her house, they made a rebellious clank as they hit the linoleum in the kitchen; then, she collapsed and began pulling up the carpet at the main entrance of the living room, its needle-felt material roughly scraped her bare knuckles like sandpaper and tore off her fingernails like loose teeth being pulled from their gums, leaving behind stains of blood on the floorboards underneath.

She fell to her side and let out several long shuddering sobs. That night, Davina Lynn had hit rock bottom. She didn't even have enough self-respect to close the door behind her; instead, she lay on the floor like a dying animal as a cold breeze occasionally swirled through the doorway and caressed her form, carrying mosquitoes that would periodically bite her ankles. She was too numb to care, let alone notice. If she didn't wake up in the morning, that would suit her just fine.

However, she did wake up in the morning, and when she did she was no longer pathetically lying on the floor, but on a comfortable divan. Her eyes felt crusty and she felt groggy as she slowly lifted herself upright, not yet comprehending that she was in a new place. When her consciousness finally did catch up to her half-opened eyes and she noticed a dazzling chandelier hanging from the ceiling, she nearly fainted.

She thought somebody must have noticed her vulnerable position last night, lying in her musty living room with the door wide open, and taken her hostage.

Before she could contemplate any further, she heard a phone ring. She reached into her pocket to pull it out, but was shocked when she noticed it wasn't in the shape of her blocky pre-paid phone. It was a legit smartphone with a smooth touchscreen. She hesitated to answer it, but noticed the caller ID read *'Dad'* along with a display of her father's picture on the screen. Without thinking too much, she tapped the prompt to answer the call and timidly spoke into the receiver.

"Hello?"

"Hey Davie," she recognized it as her dad's voice, "your mother and I are thinking about having a surprise birthday party for the boys. Is having it at the house all right, or would you and John prefer if we took them somewhere like Dave & Buster's?"

"Dad?"

"Yeah? Can you hear me? Hello?"

"Dad, is that really you?"

"What do you mean? Of course it is, honey! Who do you think it is?"

"What about the hospital? You had a heart attack."

"That's news to me." her dad chuckled. "Where'd you get that idea? Let me guess. Your mother."

"The doctor called me yesterday. I saw you hooked up to a machine in the hospital and everything."

"Honey, I don't know anything about that. You're starting to scare your old man. Is everything okay?"

Davina stood up and walked to the nearest window. She spread her index and middle fingers to pry open the horizontal slats of the window blind and peered outside with a touch of paranoia creeping up her spine. "I'm not okay. I don't know where I am, Dad. I'm trapped in some stranger's house."

"Stranger's house?! Can you get out? Should I call the cops? Do you know what street you're on?"

She squinted to make out the name on a street sign on the corner. "It looks like... Poplar Avenue."

"Poplar Avenue? Honey. That's your street. Are you at the neighbor's house?"

"I…" Davina searched through the house as she simultaneously searched for an explanation. Her eyes scanned the walls. Amid several exotic paintings she saw portraits of a family. There was a mother, father, and two young boys. "…I…" For most people, there would be nothing particularly striking about the portraits, but for Davina, it had her questioning reality itself because *she* was the mother in the portraits. "…I need to go."

"Go? I thought you were kidnapped?"

"I'm fine, Dad. I think. Can I call you back?"

"Sure, honey. I haven't had a heart attack yet, but you sure almost gave me one. Are you sure you're fine?"

"I'm sure."

"All right. Love you, Davie. Bye."

As soon as he hung up, Davina marched through the house and examined every picture, photo album, and piece of mail she could find to verify the identity of the home's residents. Each bit of evidence she compiled further convinced her that this was not a stranger's house, but her own. She was now the stranger in her own house, and she had no idea how it even happened.

Her fingers that had been scratched and bloody the night before were now manicured and clean. Her shabby house had been replaced with an upper middle class estate that might as well have been a mansion in her eyes.

A painful memory resurfaced: in her old life she had been married to a man named John Lynn, until he left her in an ugly divorce, taking their two sons with him.

Now, they were all together and living under the same roof, apparently happily. Most shockingly, but also most pleasantly, her father was still alive. Moreover, she was seemingly debt-free.

The doorbell rang, snapping her out of her chain of thoughts. She looked out through the small window panes on the side of the main door and saw her dad standing outside. He had two big bags in one hand with the phrase 'HAPPY BIRTHDAY' printed in garish colors on each of their sides. He waved and flashed a comforting smile complimented by eyes that looked concerned, as if he were telepathically pleading *please, open the door!*

Which she did. He wrapped his arms around her, giving her his signature bear hug. She could feel the bags leaning against her back. Instantly, memories came flooding back to her. Memories of growing up as an only child and receiving loads of presents at Christmastime.

Memories of her high school graduation with Pomp and Circumstance playing in the background as she giggled with her classmates and threw a peace sign back to her family in attendance.

Memories of her first date with John, and their wedding day. It was a big, yet still somehow intimate, event. After the reception, the newlywed couple slow-danced in a moonlit garden, reaffirming their vows to stay together through thick and thin.

Davina nearly burst into tears as the flow of memories came rushing into her mind. It felt as though she lived a lifetime in just the span of a few seconds.

"You had me worried, honey. What got into you on the phone earlier?" her father's voice cut through the chattering in her head. She regained her senses.

"Nothing, Dad. I just woke up from a bad dream."

"Is that all? That must've been one hell of a dream. Tell me who your dealer is, I need to avoid whatever drug they sold you."

Davina broke into laughter. She remembered now, her dad had a wicked sense of humor, if not a bit inappropriate at times, but that's what made his jokes so deliciously funny.

"Oh, these are gifts for the twins." he lifted up the gaudy bags and shook them lightly. *That's right,* Davina recalled, *I have twins: Leo and Peter.* "Your mother wants to know if you and John were planning on having the party here or somewhere else. We've been trying to get a hold of you two all week. I told her you guys were just busy, but she was getting worked up about it."

"We all can go out tonight. Peter and Leo will come back from school in an hour. John gets off at five. I can call you when we're all ready to go, probably around six thirty."

"Sounds good. Should I leave the bags here, or–?"

"Put them in your trunk. I don't want to be held responsible if they get lost."

"All right. Well, I was just checking on you. Glad you're safe and not trapped in somebody's basement."

Davina smirked and shook her head. "Thanks for checking in, Dad."

He smiled and nodded. "That's my job. Official

Checker-Inner." He walked back to the door. "Just give us a call in a few hours or whenever you're ready." And with that final reminder, he left.

Davina watched him shuffle back to his Buick Lacrosse. He was spry for an old guy, but she could see some effects of aging creeping in – a slight limp in his steps, and a faint hunch in his posture. Still, at least he was alive and kicking. This wasn't a bad reality at all.

She may have been easing into her new life. She may have nearly forgotten all of the painful memories of her alternative past the way one forgets a dream. But there was one detail that had been branded into her temporal lobes: she had been called to Montgomery Memorial Hospital and had seen her father dead. That had happened just as sure as her name was Davina Lynn. As sure as the sky was blue. Her father *had* died and she *had* been his sole surviving family member.

She knew it was best not to think about it, that she'd be better off not questioning anything, for her own peace of mind at least. She knew she should be thankful for her life and all the blessings in it.

So she kept quiet and hoped that this specific memory in her mind would one day disappear and turn out to be false after all. She took her family out to a local pizza place that had an arcade and celebrated the twelfth birthday of her twin sons. To the outside world she looked like just a normal mom. No one could have imagined the torturous thoughts lingering in the back of her mind.

For a while, she was able to lead an ordinary life as a

housewife. She did all the usual household chores, but also had a small business writing online articles for her housekeeping blog on the side. The ad revenue alone was enough to pay for all the groceries each month, but she didn't do it for the money – she did it to keep her mind off of her single biggest fear in life.

The fear of her current reality being a mere dream. The fear of going back to her old reality, destitute and poor, on the verge of being homeless. The fear of losing her dad.

This fear led her to researching her experience. The experience of having a clear memory in her head that did not match up with the reality she was living. Could it have been a realistic dream? Had it been a past life, perhaps?

Her limited investigation led to her discovery of a phenomena known as a *false memory*, otherwise known as the 'Mandela Effect' which earned its name from one of the most well-known false memories wherein the memory not only affected an individual but an entire population of people – a collective false memory. This was a memory of the late South African leader Nelson Mandela. Although he died in 2013, many people thought he had actually died in the 1980s. Not only did they mistakenly think he had died when he hadn't, they had vivid memories of news reports of his death that more or less correlated with one another – down to the time and cause of death. There were many other examples of collective false memories, but none of them were taken very seriously by the general public. Most people saw it as just a simple misconstruction of memory, like an ugly cousin of déjà vu, probably caused by hearing a rumor repeated or accidentally re-enforcing a misunderstanding enough times until it became baked into one's own consciousness.

For individual false memories, the prevailing logic was that they were caused by the repression of painful memories, leading to a constructed reality – a safe mental haven – for one to turn to in times of stress.

But this didn't adequately explain Davina's situation. She wasn't blocking a painful memory. If anything, she wished she *could* block the 'false' memory that she had for causing her so much pain.

Living under this dark and lonely cloud started to have an even more negative impact on her. She began to drink alcohol on a daily basis. It started off innocent enough, just a glass of wine a day, but quickly escalated until she was, by all accounts, a closet alcoholic. This habit eventually started taking a toll on her marriage and family life.

Her husband and sons attempted an intervention. They presented all kinds of evidence, from broken picture frames, to vomit-soiled laundry, and citing her increasingly frequent mood swings. Her twins recounted coming home to her passed out in the bathroom, head hanging over the toilet, and her husband added that she had been spending an ungodly sum of money on booze every month. Through it all, Davina was defensive and in outright denial.

"Don't you understand!" she cried, "I'm not from

this world! Daddy died! I'm not supposed to be here! All of this—" she motioned around the house with exaggerated hand movements, "—isn't real! It's not real... Nothing is..."

Due to her stubborn insistence, the rest of the family learned to live with her emotional outbursts and often unpredictable behavior. They stood by and silently watched as she transformed from a highly functional woman into a train wreck over the course of a year. It was their belief that she would only change when she decided to on her own terms; until then, there was little they could do other than continue loving and supporting her.

She was too numb to feel their love and support though, so she sought it out elsewhere. She turned to online chat rooms and quickly found a man willing to take her mind off of things when they both had some spare time and their families were away. He would come by the house after John left for work in the morning and the twins were at school. Ironically, for meeting in a chat room, her and her secret lover rarely talked. Like the alcohol, she didn't turn to him for anything healthy, only for some semblance of solace – a way to distract herself. Their interactions were purely physical in nature.

It didn't take long for John to find out about her hidden affair. Not that she went through great pains to hide it. This sordid revelation only served to further break down their once happy marriage.

After several months of failed couples therapy sessions, John finally filed for divorce. Legally, due to her alcoholism and affair, Davina was not eligible for much in terms of alimony. More devastatingly, she lost custody of both of her sons.

In that chaotic period of dysfunction, there was only one person left who still had her back. That one person was her father. He was there for her, paying for all of her rehabilitation and even buying her a small house to live in until she could get back on her feet. He invested so much into her that he didn't have much money left when her mother received an unfortunate and untimely diagnosis of Stage IV pancreatic cancer. She died shortly thereafter.

Some say that it was the death of his wife that caused his broken heart to ultimately suffer from major complications leading to him checking into Montgomery Memorial Hospital one bleak Friday afternoon..

Davina was sitting in a wooden swing on her front porch when she got a call from his doctor the following Wednesday.

HUMPBACK

As the population of whales on Earth steadily declined in the 21st century, many environmental scientists warned of the implications. They called for the practice of whaling to come to an end, and for the international community to work together towards cleaning the polluted oceans of the world. Despite these calls for reasonable measures, none were taken, and the number of whales plummeted to a level of near extinction.

Most of the concern was for larger species of whale that purportedly served a similarly larger role in maintaining the ecosystem of not only the marine world, but the world on land as well.

The accepted science was that these larger species of whales, such as humpbacks and blue whales, were a driving force in the natural growth of phytoplankton in the ocean. Research indicated that whale feces fertilized plankton, and that the movement of water caused by whales traveling through the ocean helped push growing plankton back up into the photic zone (the area of the ocean that is closest to the surface) where it could survive and serve as food for other marine animals. Additionally, plant plankton was believed to absorb massive amounts of carbon dioxide. In those days, carbon dioxide was a major contributor towards climate change, and anything that helped reduce the levels of carbon in the atmosphere was considered immensely useful.

Due to all of these reasons, you can imagine the panic that set in when whale populations were bordering on being non-existent. The effects rippled throughout the food chain. With less plankton there was less food for other aquatic life, thus many species of fish became extinct, leading to even less food resources for human consumption. The threat of increased carbon levels was just poison icing on the cake.

Governments the world over worked around the clock to find a solution to the lack of whales.

Initiating breeding programs for whales in nature or even captivity was deemed too time-consuming and costly. It didn't take long for the world's top scientific minds, corporations, and politicians to reach consensus on a solution that could potentially solve the problem in a quick manner. That solution was to create a species of genetically engineered whales. Instead of waiting twelve months to raise a handful of whale calves to young adulthood that may or may not survive, they determined that creating large groups of fully grown whales in a lab in a few months would be more efficient and cost effective.

These lab-grown whales were created from the DNA of humpback whales and were expected to be released into the wild where they would, theoretically, live like normal whales with all the same contributions to the ecosystem.

Early on in the plan, unforeseeable issues began to arise; primarily that the genetically engineered whales did not always share traits with their natural counterparts. Some of them exhibited behavioral differences that drastically diverged from normal humpback behavior.

A few caretakers assigned to the project began to feel wary of getting close enough to some of the cloned whales during feeding time. Although the whales were contained within secure water-filled repositories, some of them would violently wriggle when approached. Occasionally, this movement dislodged the repositories they were being held in. In some instances this led to the injury and even death of several caretakers.

Due to a particular whale's powerful movements, one individual lost his footing while trying to administer food tubes into the repository. He fell into the repository and was pulled under by the angry whale until he drowned.

Another caretaker was outright decapitated by a whale that thrust itself just far enough out of its tubular container to clamp its jaws down on her head as she was leaning over an observation deck to check the temperature gauge for the repositories.

These incidents, and many others, were chalked up to the nature and scope of the project. Overseers of the operation considered most of these occurrences to be nothing more than freak accidents. Besides, certain risks were expected to be involved in such an environment either way. The number of incidences was considered to be within an acceptable range.

The only thing that gave pause to some of those behind the project was the rapid mutation some of the whales displayed. The most common mutation was the gradual replacement of the counterfeit humpbacks' bristles with legitimate teeth – not just teeth but an actual set of jaws. Shark-like jaws. Jaws for cutting through flesh instead of holding in krill.

Other mutations included deformed appendages protruding from random areas on certain whales' bodies and compound eyes growing on top of their heads.

All of the mutated whales were euthanized. It was hoped that this would weed out the potential for unwanted mutations in the future. Those involved in the large-scale experiment assumed the mutations were a byproduct of faulty programming in some of the whale's genomes, similar to birth defects present in the natural world. As with every other misstep, these were viewed as unfortunate but explainable byproducts of the work itself. Creating life from scratch is messy business, after all.

They soon discovered just how messy a business it could be after releasing several dozen of the fully grown artificial whales into the Atlantic Ocean. In the beginning, the results were promising; the whales were interacting normally with their environment. They were producing fecal matter on par with normal humpbacks and certain populations of fish seemed to be increasing as a result. The man-made humpbacks were also reproducing with normal humpbacks, and their offspring were considered to be healthy.

Sadly, the positive results were short-lived. Within a few years, the original team of fake humpbacks had degenerated into ghastly creatures unrecognizable from their former selves. Their gray, bumpy skin had turned ghost-white and squishy; not only that, but their eyes somehow gravitated to the tips of their noses, as though they acquired new faces in the front, and these eyes were sunken in by deep pockets. Their eye sockets also expanded into large and perfectly round circles.

And those jaws... those horrible jaws that were thought to have been eliminated with the destruction of the previous defective whales, returned. Sometimes protruding outward like those of an angler fish.

Most concerning were the extra limbs they grew. While these limbs were seen as nothing but non-functional attachments at first, or benign tumors, they slowly became just as functional as the whale's flippers. Some of these extra limbs resembled webbed hands attached to long, spindly arms that the whales dragged behind themselves like a caveman might drag his club. And just as a caveman would use his club, so did the whales use their newfound accessories. They were known to grab prey with their hideous hands, sometimes even reaching out of the water and plucking seagulls flying low enough to the ocean's surface.

Often, these abominable creatures would die of most likely unnatural causes and wash ashore, scarring the impressionable minds of young children and adults alike with their repulsive physical features.

Despite flaws in their genetic code, the beasts proved to be adept at two things: reproducing and killing. They reproduced like rabbits and aged at an astonishing rate. Within three weeks of birth, one of their calves could be the size of a full-grown adult humpback. Their gestation period was also remarkably short; whereas most humpbacks were in the womb for at least eleven months before birth, the fetus of one of these genetically engineered whales could be conceived and born within two months.

Needless to say, they rapidly evolved into the ocean's dominant apex predator, surpassing great whites and orcas. But unlike other apex predators, they showed no reservations about eating humans. While attacks on humans from other sea animals were relatively rare, the killer humpbacks seemed to prefer eating human flesh. They frequently swam close to shorelines where large groups of people gathered and would systematically use their slimy, mutated hands to snatch unsuspecting swimmers and slowly eat them feet first. Dying at the hands of one of them was said to be one of the most agonizing deaths one could endure. They intentionally prolonged their victims' deaths because they preferred their food to be alive and suffering, especially humans. The creatures seemed to know not to hold humans below water for too long as to prevent drowning. They would often lift their victims above water for air before pulling them back down over and over again to finish feasting.

As terrifying as all this sounds, it was merely a precursor of things to come. The next step the humpbacks took in their mad dash of an evolutionary process was far more chilling than anyone could have predicted. To even speak its name is to invite misfortune of immense magnitude into one's life.

Very few are still alive who can recall the origins of the tyrannical behemoths that currently share this world with us. But I recall. And I write this today to not only preserve the unbelievable story of our past, but to implore anyone who might read this to find a better way to solve this nightmarish predicament than the solution our ancestors created. What they created were monsters.

Perhaps this is the end of humanity, our destiny – to become victims of our own creation. I certainly hope not, but with each passing day that seems to be the case. They're outside now, I can hear them bellowing in the distance.

Please, if you find this... please, do not repeat the follies of our ancestors. Do not get so lost in your aspirations to make the world a better place that you plunge it into the darkness which I will soon find myself in.

MUSINGS FROM THE UNDERWORLD:
Words from the Author

Reading has a been staple of my life since I sounded out my first vowel, but my writing journey didn't really begin until high school. My high school years marked the first time my work was published. Not my pure written words, but my own comic strip that I wrote and illustrated, which was printed weekly in the local newspaper. It was both a breakthrough and a sign of things to come.

Most comic strips, be they print-based or digital-based, typically fall under the comedy genre. Thus, the years I spent drawing and writing comics were largely devoted to comedy.

There's a funny thing about comedy, though (pun intended), which is that its closest relative in the realm of entertainment is horror. More than any other two genres, these two share common obstacles and goals. When writing comedy one must dive into his or her own sense of humor and ponder a few things: what makes people laugh? What is funny to most people? What humorous observations about daily life can I make that no one else has?

Horror is similar, but instead of trying to uncover what makes you laugh, it tries to uncover what makes you scream. What are you scared of? What keeps you up at night? What terrifying observations about daily life can be made that no one else has noticed before?

I, like millions of other people, have always been

attracted to the horror aesthetic. As a kid, being scared was not an enjoyable experience for me; however, as I grew older I formed a sort of nostalgia for that old sense of fear. Beyond the nostalgia, I thought re-evaluating my old fears could be an interesting peephole into my own inner psychology and a way to better understand myself.

Which is true – the more I conquered my old fears and understood why I had them, the more I became in tune to my true self over time. Later, I'd use these same introspective skills to help others understand not just what they were scared of but *why* they were scared of it.

These cathartic experiences led me to consider branching out and publishing horror stories.

I set out to writing and finishing *Suburbs of the Underworld* in the span of one month. My goal was to write as many short horror stories as I reasonably could under this time limit. Some of the stories dip into comedy or sci-fi, but they all still fall somewhere under the horror umbrella.

For this book, my main source of horror came from the unknown; more specifically, the unknown from within oneself. I wanted to put a spotlight on some of the uglier aspects of the human psyche and show what one might be capable of when put in a certain situation. A few of these are cautionary tales so that if you find yourself in circumstances that may run parallel to those described in this book (minus the supernatural elements), you don't succumb to your darker side.

Horror stories do not often give us role models. Role models serve as examples of what to do in a given situation. On the contrary, characters in horror stories generally serve as examples of what *not* to do in a given situation. They are usually the exact opposite of role models.

A lot of entertainment aims to show humanity at its finest and gives us examples of what to strive for. They feed into our ego. Comedy and horror are the uninvited guests at the dinner table that exist to remind us of our flaws. They keep our hubris in check. Horror, in particular.

Many of the stories in this book describe a world where our human fears have, intentionally or inadvertently, physically manifested themselves into reality. Some of the fears are justifiable, some of them are not, yet all of them – left to fester – take on a life of their own. It's a *damned if you do, damned if you don't* world, not so different from our own.

I hope reading it felt like driving through a stretch of familiar suburbs. Suburbs that you've perhaps visited before, in your dreams. *Suburbs of the Underworld.*

— Cyrus G. Oliver II